My uncle Rafe has done some really weird things in his time but using me to pick up an attractive woman really was too much, as I tried to point out to him. But would he listen to me? What do you think?

Actually, I could see his point. I was impressed with Ashley, myself. Of course, it was immediately obvious to me that she didn't know a thing about babies. But I'm a patient sort, and her heart was in the right place.

More important, it gave Uncle Rafe a chance to get to know her better. Talk about a smooth operator. She never knew what hit her. The next thing she knew he had her right where he wanted her.

I must say I was pleased with my part in the whole affair.

Baby Josh

Please address questions and book requests to: Silhouette Reader Service
U.S.: 3010 Walden Ave., P.O. Box 1325, Buffalo, NY 14269
Canadian: P.O. Box 609, Fort Erie, Ont. L2A 5X3

Instant Families

ANNETTE
BROADRICK
CIRCUMSTANTIAL EVIDENCE

Silhouette Books

Published by Silhouette Books
America's Publisher of Contemporary Romance

SILHOUETTE BOOKS
300 East 42nd St.,
New York, N.Y. 10017

ISBN 0-373-30113-8

CIRCUMSTANTIAL EVIDENCE

Copyright © 1984 by Annette Broadrick

Celebrity Wedding Certificates published by permission of Donald Ray Pounders from *Celebrity Wedding Ceremonies.*

This edition published by arrangement with Harlequin Books S.A.

® and TM are trademarks of Harlequin Books S.A., used under license. Trademarks indicated with ® are registered in the United States Patent and Trademark Office, the Canadian Trade Marks Office and in other countries.

Printed in U.S.A.

A Letter from the Author

Dear Reader,

A first book, like a first love, is very special and can never be forgotten.

Circumstantial Evidence was my first book, the one that I wrote never really believing it would make it into print or be seen by anyone. You can imagine how delighted I am that Silhouette has chosen to reissue it in their HERE COME THE GROOMS series.

My manuscript was unsolicited. In those days, such manuscripts were sent to professional readers to review. The first person to read my manuscript later joined the publisher's staff full-time and a few years later became my editor. Tara Gavin and I have worked together now for ten years.

Circumstantial Evidence was my first book, Tara was the first publisher's representative to read it. Her enthusiasm for my work since then has kept me going when I might have otherwise faltered and stopped writing.

This is a story that kept popping into my head until I was forced to put it down on paper. What a strange idea, after all—a good-looking stranger places a baby in your arms and acts as though the two of you are married?

And then what happens…? And so the story began. I hope you'll enjoy it.

Sincerely,

Annette Broadrick

To Lynn and Lauraine, who insisted...

Chapter One

Ashley Allison glanced at the digital watch on her wrist—*7:15*—and decided to forget about staying at the office until she cleared her desk. Her body felt as though she'd spent the day working out in a gym, rather than in court.

Her watch continued to flash other information—month, *June;* day, *Friday;* date, *28*—which she ignored. She was already aware of the date. She'd spent six hours on trial at the Multnomah County Courthouse in Portland, Oregon, and even the fact that she'd won couldn't compensate for the energy she'd expended.

The framed print hanging on the wall in front of her desk caught her eye as she stood up and stretched. It was a cartoonist's version of Ashley's home state, Texas. The exaggerated shape stretched as far north as the Great Lakes, east to Maine, and west to California. The print had been solemnly presented to her by the staff on her twenty-eighth birthday in November.

No one in the office allowed her to forget her origin, her southern drawl, or her nickname—"long, tall Texan." Since Ashley stood five feet eight inches in her bare feet, she couldn't argue with the nickname—or the sentiment: *If you're born a Texan, you never recover.*

Ashley pushed her shoulder-length hair behind her ears as she reached for her briefcase. Unloading papers taken to court, she glanced at the stacks of files and correspondence scattered across her desk and tried to decide what work to take home. No. She intended to forget all about the law for the next couple of days and enjoy some of the rare sunshine they'd been having. She glanced out of her window and saw Mount Hood shimmering white against the blue sky. She might even drive up into the mountains tomorrow and enjoy the fresh air.

Her thoughts turned to possible plans for the evening. She had refused an invitation to see the musical comedy at the Civic Auditorium that night. One of the new associates had invited her to go, but she didn't want to encourage his interest. How many times had she explained to various men that she had no time to devote to a relationship, that her career took too much of her time and energy? Yet there always seemed to be some egotistical male who was convinced he could change her mind and whisk her away from the drudgery of the legal world.

"There's no such critter," Ashley muttered, and her mind suddenly flashed to the image of a man she'd seen that morning in the elevator. She'd never seen him before, she was certain of that. His looks were not the type a person would forget. For one thing, his size made him quite noticeable. Even in her two-inch heels Ashley found herself looking up several inches to meet his eyes. Those eyes were what had caught her attention. In a deeply bronzed face, their silver blue was striking. His ebony hair suggested that his skin tones were natural rather than the result of long exposure to the sun. So where had he gotten those eyes?

It would take more than a pair of unforgettable blue eyes, however, to cause Ashley to stray from her chosen course. She hoped to become a partner in the law firm of Begley, Henderson & Howe by the time she reached thirty, and no man, regardless of wealth, charm, or beautiful eyes, could offer anything more appealing to Ashley. Still—she'd never seen eyes quite like his before. Funny she should remember them.

As she left the office she wondered what Tasha might have in store for her that night. She loved her Siamese cat dearly but admitted that she could be a real pain. Tasha hated being left alone nights. Normally, Ashley had no problem with that idiosyncrasy since she seldom stayed out late, but that week had been an exception. Monday she'd attended an Oregon Symphony concert with a friend, and when she had arrived home she was ignored by her cat instead of being greeted with a recounting of the day's events. On Wednesday Ashley had arrived home after a long day to find her living room strewn with papers and magazines that she'd left stacked in a neat pile on the coffee table. Instead of the stack, the table held a sleek and satisfied-looking Siamese cat in the midst of intricate ablutions. Ashley dreaded to think of what Tasha might have dreamed up as punishment for that night.

As she started down the hallway to the elevators, Ashley was already planning her evening. She could hardly wait to kick off her shoes, pour herself a large glass of wine, and relax in a hot bath.

In another office on the same floor Raphael McCord had his own problems. While leaving telephone instructions with his assistant in San Francisco, he was interrupted by a strange man who burst into the office with a degree of belligerence seldom seen in the business world.

McCord kept an eye on the short, beefy man, noting the deep frown marring his face, as he continued to speak into the telephone.

"That's about it, Jim. I should be arriving on the 9:05 flight on Monday, so have the car at the airport. I'll see you then." He hung up the phone and studied the man in front of him. A green and yellow plaid jacket strained across the protruding stomach and partially revealed the open collar of a dingy white shirt. Clenched fists hung below frayed cuffs. McCord cocked an eyebrow and gazed into eyes that looked like brown marbles decorated with red lace. "Is there something I can do for you?" McCord's tone implied that he doubted it.

"Your name McCord?" the man asked. Since the name on the office door read *McCord Industries*, he could be excused for jumping to conclusions.

"That's right."

A beefy hand shot out across the desk. "I'm Pete Wilson. Virgil Tysinger sent me." He waited as though he'd just explained all that was necessary.

A slight frown appeared on McCord's face. "Why?" he asked, shaking the extended paw with some reluctance.

That must have been the wrong question. Wilson's face turned a deeper shade of red and the veins in his beefy neck began to stand out. "Don't play games with me, McCord. He wants you and your wife to have dinner with him tonight. He told me to come by and pick you up." His frown deepened. "You'd never be able to find the place on your own."

McCord started at the word *wife.* His brief glance at the sofa by the windows confirmed that the infant still slept. Wilson intercepted the glance and spotted the baby.

"Where's your wife?"

McCord needed time to think, but he had none. He gave Wilson an appraising stare, then came to his feet in a lazy manner, towering over the other man. "She's shopping at the moment. We're supposed to meet later." He motioned to the baby. "As you can see, I'm baby-sitting."

"When are you supposed to meet her?"

McCord glanced down at his watch in an effort to stall for time. Seven-fifteen. Later than he thought. He shrugged as he moved toward the baby. "You know what women are like. There's no telling."

"Then we'd better locate her. It takes a while to get to Tysinger's place." He edged to the window and glanced out. "Which direction did she take?"

McCord picked up the infant and grabbed its diaper bag. "I'm not sure. I think she said she'd meet me at the car."

"Then let's get down there. The sooner we find her, the sooner we can get started." The man had a positive genius for overstating the obvious.

"Look, Mr. Wilson." McCord used his most reasonable tone. "I appreciate the invitation, but let's make it for some other time, okay?" He ushered Wilson out of the office, made sure the door locked behind him, and motioned Wilson down the hall to the elevators. He wasn't sure what he was going to do when Wilson discovered there was no wife waiting at the car. He'd think of something, he supposed. This wasn't the first time he'd managed to bluff himself out of a situation not of his making.

The sound of an angry male voice reached Ashley as she rounded the corner near the elevators. An inner alarm jangled. She knew that most people who worked in the building had gone home long before.

Two men stood near the elevators; a short, heavy-set man was doing most of the talking. Her concern eased when she recognized the man listening to the tirade. He was her elevator companion of the morning, the one with the unforgettable blue eyes. Ashley watched with amusement. He seemed to have his hands full with an irate client. Then the shorter man moved a pace to the side and Ashley discovered that "Blue Eyes" literally had his hands full. He held an infant tucked into his arm much as a football player would carry a ball, and he had a diaper bag dangling from his other hand.

The business suit and diaper bag didn't blend too well, in Ashley's opinion, although the baby seemed content enough. *Better him than me. Give me a brief over a bassinet any day.*

The elevator made its appearance, and Ashley moved toward the lighted area near the men. She'd be home in a matter of minutes. It couldn't be too soon for her.

As she stepped into the elevator, Ashley nodded to the man she recognized, giving him a tentative smile. The short man spun around and saw her at the same time his companion spoke.

"Oh, there you are, love. I thought we were supposed to meet back at the car."

Ashley glanced around, wondering whom he'd addressed in such familiar terms. There was no one else in the elevator, and he was staring at her. Her smile wavered. Perhaps she had misunderstood him. There was no way she could misunderstand his next actions. He approached her and with a deft movement transferred the small infant from his arms to hers. He leaned over and kissed the side of her mouth as he murmured, "I think Josh missed you almost as much as I did."

Ashley blinked as she glanced down at the baby thrust into her arms. He returned her look with a solemn, blue-eyed inspection. The man at her side pulled her close to him.

"I want you to meet my wife, Mr. Wilson." He smiled at her and added in a warm tone, "Honey, this is Pete Wilson. He dropped in rather unexpectedly today." Ashley stared at the two men as the incredible conversation continued. "He's brought us an invitation from Virgil Tysinger for dinner tonight." His expression reflected his regret. "I explained to him that we've already made plans for the evening." In a cordial tone he addressed Wilson once again. "Maybe we can get together with Tysinger some time next week."

My God! They must be filming a television series here in the building and I got on the wrong elevator. But surely these men knew she wasn't part of the production, didn't they? The name Virgil Tysinger registered. What would the state legislator have to do with all of this?

Ashley managed to get her tongue unglued from the roof of her mouth. "I think there's been some sort of mistake—"

The man introduced as Pete Wilson interrupted. "Look here, McCord, I told you—Tysinger doesn't care what your plans are, he wants to see you—" The elevator doors opened onto the lobby.

McCord's arm clamped around Ashley's waist and he guided her into the marbled lobby. She looked around, her first thought centered on getting the guard's attention. As they reached the front door, McCord spoke to the man on duty.

"Goodnight, Sam. Have a good weekend."

"You too, Mr. McCord." His smile of acknowledgement did not register anything unusual in the departure of the three adults and infant.

Ashley's adrenalin managed to overcome the inertia caused by her shock. "Just a blasted minute. What do you think you're doing?" She planted her feet, determined not to move another step. The two men paused, similar expressions of impatience darting across dissimilar countenances.

"I've already explained to Wilson that we can't make the dinner tonight, honey. I don't understand his insistence any more than you do." McCord's glance at Wilson would have wilted a less determined man.

Shaking her head in an unconscious attempt to make sense out of a senseless statement, Ashley attempted her most calm, dispassionate, courtroom voice. "I don't have the faintest idea of what you're talking about. I've never seen you before in my life." Not a totally accurate statement, perhaps, but close enough to make her point.

"What do you mean, you've never seen me before? What kind of a silly statement is that? You married me, didn't you, or is that up for debate as well?"

Ashley's well-ordered, uncomplicated existence began to unravel. Had she stepped into some sort of time warp?

"Married? Are you out of your mind? I certainly am not married." Her firm denunciation was made in ringing tones of sincerity that would have convinced a jury anywhere.

"I suppose you're also going to deny that Josh is our son?" He indicated the infant in her arms with all the drama of a prosecuting attorney exhibiting the murder weapon to the jury.

"Our son!" Ashley's conversation had degenerated to repeating parts of his sentences. She stared with a certain amount of horror into the eyes of the young person in her arms and was rewarded with a smile that seemed to have been produced on cue.

Wilson stepped toward them, menace in every line of his body. "Look, McCord. We don't have time for this. You and the missus can fight in the car as well as here on the steps. Get going." He spun around and started down the steps in front of them.

What an unpleasant person, Ashley thought, a faint tremor coursing through her body. Not exactly a first choice for a lighthearted companion. She had no idea what was going on, but knew darned well she wanted no part of it.

She turned to McCord and held out the baby. "I'm not going anywhere with either of you, do you understand me? If you don't leave me alone, I'll scream my head off until every policeman in downtown Portland will think a riot's taking place." She glared at him with all the anger, indignation, and fear that had been building within her.

Unfortunately McCord wasn't intimidated, nor was he accepting the baby she offered him. Instead he propelled them both down the steps and started leading Ashley past the other man with a brusque "We've got to go" to Wilson.

Ashley heard Wilson say, "Sorry, McCord, I only obey orders, and my orders was to get you and the missus and bring you to Tysinger." Then she saw two more men materialize before them, effectively blocking their path. Ashley's heart leaped from its normal position in her chest to play Ping Pong between her throat and her stomach. These men didn't have to work at looking intimidating. Almost identical in build, their arms bulged with well-developed biceps that would give the Incredible Hulk competition. She had no desire to see how they behaved when angry.

McCord's voice sent a chill through Ashley, though he never raised his tone. "I don't care for your strong-arm tactics, Wilson. I don't like threats, either against me or my family. My wife and I have other plans. Now get your playmates to move out of the way.''

Once again McCord and Ashley moved forward, this time with Ashley's full consent and approval. Then she saw the long, low limousine illegally parked at the curb, a rear door open. With the three men surrounding them, McCord and Ashley had no escape route open.

One of the trained primates muttered, ''Get in, McCord, we've wasted enough time. We don't want trouble, but if you're gonna insist, we'll oblige.''

Ashley's ability to think on her feet, a necessary trait for a good trial lawyer, deserted her in her time of need. She'd never been physically overwhelmed before.

McCord's arm tightened and Ashley glanced up at him. He stared into her eyes as though attempting to read her thoughts. She returned his gaze, refusing to allow him to see her fear. McCord touched her cheek gently with his finger. ''We might as well see what this is all about.'' He took the baby from her, assisted Ashley into the limousine, and climbed in behind her. The other men wasted no time; two of them leaped into the front seat, and Wilson got into the back with Ashley and McCord.

The last door slammed and the limousine pulled silently away from the curb, gathering speed as it neared the Hawthorne Bridge and crossed the Willamette River.

McCord handed the baby back to Ashley, reached into the bag he still carried, and brought out a bottle, saying, "Josh hasn't been fed." He handed her the bottle. Ashley studied his face, searching for a clue as to what was happening. Then she looked at the infant in her arms, who was already anticipating the delights of the bottle in front of him. He seemed to know what to do with it as she stuck it with some awkwardness into his mouth. What Ashley knew about babies could be inscribed on the heel of one of her two-inch pumps, with plenty of room to spare. However, the infant didn't appear to need much instruction at the moment. He grasped the bottle as though afraid she'd try to remove it.

McCord spoke to the man seated beside him. "Look, I don't know what this is all about, but I'm willing to go see Tysinger if you'll just drop my wife and son off at home."

Why did he insist on their marital relationship? Other than a rather bizarre insistence on claiming a stranger to be his wife, the man appeared strikingly normal. Ordinarily Ashley would have considered him a man who could be depended upon in any situation. She wouldn't feel in the least unsure of his ability to cope if he'd just drop the myth of their relationship. So he had made a mistake. No one was perfect. Why didn't he just admit it and get her out of this mess?

Wilson's tone reflected an unexpected apology. "I'm sorry about all of this, McCord. But the invitation was for you and your wife. Tysinger insisted on that. I'm sure this whole thing is some kind of misunderstanding he'll clear up when you see him." He drew a once white handkerchief from his back pocket and wiped away the beads of perspiration glistening on his forehead. The day wasn't particularly warm.

Ashley leaned forward. "Are you talking about Virgil Tysinger, the state representative?"

Wilson nodded with unfeigned eagerness to make amends. "That's right."

"Is this some new type of campaign strategy, dragging people off the streets for a meal? Because if it is, someone should convince him there are more subtle methods for getting reelected."

McCord covered a sudden chuckle with a cough, as Wilson's flushed face turned a darker hue.

"Miz McCord, I'm sure Mr. Tysinger will be able to explain everything once we get there."

"Get where, Mr. Wilson?" Ashley's tone was deceptively gentle.

"Huh?"

"Get where, Mr. Wilson?" she repeated even more gently. "Where are you taking us?" Anyone who knew Ashley would have recognized the tone that denoted a slow rage building. Unfortunately, Wilson accepted the sweetness at its face value.

"Oh! Well, Mr. Tysinger thought you'd like to visit his mountain retreat in the Cascades. He's got a real nice place and tries to spend as much of his free time there as possible." Wilson's premature smile of relief disappeared with Ashley's next comment.

"Mr. Wilson, what you have just done constitutes kidnapping, and state representative or not, Virgil Tysinger is an accessory. Kidnapping is a federal offense, Mr. Wilson. If you're ever going to have an original thought in your head, I strongly advise you to have it now and not leave the city limits of Portland with us in this car. Federal prisons are not known for their hospitality." Her tone stayed soft, but there was no doubt in anyone's mind that she was furious.

Turning to glare at the man sitting next to her, Ashley said in the same tone, "Would you care to explain to me why you've insisted that I am your wife?"

McCord's eyes glinted in the afternoon light. "Well, for one thing, it proves Josh's legitimacy."

"Are you trying to be funny?" she demanded.

"Not particularly. I just don't know any other way to answer your question."

"My question is not that difficult, Mr. McCord. But let me rephrase it for you. I—" she pointed with some gravity to herself "—am not married. Nor do I have any children. Why, then, are you insisting that I am married to you, and that this baby is ours?"

McCord studied the young woman seated by his side. *So what do you do now, McCord? You and your sudden impulse to help others seems to have backfired.* His gaze took in Ashley's large, luminous eyes, the softness of a mouth that managed to portray sensitivity even when clamped in anger, and the cinnamon hair that fell in waves from a central part to frame her face. She ignored his inspection as he took in her tailored suit and the curving shape it covered. McCord fell back on a habit that had worked well for him in the past. If you don't know what to say to them, kiss 'em. So he did.

His movement caught her off guard and she froze as his mouth moved across hers in a warm caress. The baby in her arms prevented her from resisting the sudden move. However, the unexpectedness of the kiss wasn't the only thing that startled her into immobility. What caught Ashley completely off guard was the sudden burst of intense feeling generated within her when McCord moved his mouth lazily across hers. The kiss was almost playful—an exploration of possible joys to be found, a willingness to indulge in a get-acquainted meeting. Then his mouth settled more firmly against hers, his tongue flicking across her bottom lip in an audacious search for intimacy. Had the sensation he created not been so enticing, Ashley would have described it as almost an electrical shock, or something like the static shock one got from walking across carpeting and then touching metal. Her eyes fluttered closed in an unconscious effort to recognize and identify the reaction caused by the kiss.

Once again the technique worked for McCord. Ashley forgot her question. In fact, for a short while she forgot that she was in a large automobile with several strangers, being whisked to some unknown destination for unspecified purposes. The question that surfaced after a brief spell was even more pressing. *Who was this man and how can he have such an effect on me?*

There was no way of knowing how long Ashley would have sat there contemplating the newest discovery she'd made about herself if nature hadn't suddenly taken over. Her small charge had managed to drain his bottle and then thoroughly soak his diaper. Ashley looked at McCord with a hint of panic in her eyes. She leaned over and spoke in a low tone. "He's wet."

McCord glanced past Ashley to the expanse of velour cushion between her and the door. "You've got room to change him, haven't you?"

Fighting to maintain her decorum, Ashley responded through clenched teeth. "He's *your* baby. You change him!"

McCord's grin was the first Ashley had seen since she'd walked up to the elevators. Only by relaxing did McCord give away how tense he'd been. For some reason her reaction to the baby's condition amused him. His amusement increased her disgust. He reached into the bag and brought out a disposable diaper while Ashley sat there, a most unfeminine glare on her face. She stared at the disposable diaper, then at him, and at last down at the helpless infant. What was she doing here? She wouldn't even have *recognized* a disposable diaper if she hadn't seen them advertised on television. Josh gazed up at her with trusting blue eyes and popped two middle fingers into his mouth as he waited with infinite patience for her help.

Setting her jaw, she snatched the offending object from McCord's grasp. Turning to the innocent baby, she mentally apologized for being so personal on such short acquaintance and managed to secure the dry diaper on him without undue awkwardness.

Baby care was not part of the law school curriculum. Just wait until she had an opportunity to give this arrogant example of macho manhood her views of the male population in general and of him in particular.

Ashley picked up the baby and laid him with some trepidation against her shoulder. Would he be willing to be this close to her? Obviously so, because he snuggled his face into her neck and relaxed. So this mixture of delicately scented powder and warm body was a baby. Such a trusting scrap of humanity. Dry clothes, full tummy, and a shoulder to sleep on—he really didn't ask for much, but she knew from her moment of panic that she'd reached her limits of adaptability. Whether he liked it or not, McCord was going to have to take over the role of parent when the baby awakened.

More than an hour had gone by since they'd left downtown Portland. They were already on the winding mountain roads, and Ashley had no idea when they'd left the main highway—her thoughts had kept her preoccupied. At the moment she conceded that she had no option but to wait until they reached Tysinger. She began to rehearse what she'd say to the man. She was determined to get back to Portland immediately, his dinner plans notwithstanding.

Her thoughts returned to Tasha and she stiffened. The thought of what she'd find when she finally managed to reach home made her shudder.

It was almost enough to make her wish she'd stayed in Texas.

Chapter Two

After they had bounced over miles of jarring roads that grew worse the higher they climbed, their automobile made a sharp turn and came to an abrupt halt in a clearing. Ashley and Josh would have been thrown forward if McCord's quick reflexes hadn't stopped them.

Ashley could see no sign of a dwelling but stepped out when the door next to her opened. McCord was right behind her, his hand resting in the small of her back. A trail disappeared around a turn at the edge of the clearing, and Wilson motioned to them to follow the men into the woods. Ashley glanced down at her shoes and shook her head. She'd be lucky not to sprain an ankle, or worse. She tried not to think about it as McCord's arm came around her waist for support. She wasn't ready to ignore his help as they followed their escorts up a steep grade.

When they reached the top of the ridge, Ashley caught her breath. On the other side the ground dropped abruptly a few hundred feet to a large lake that reflected a gleaming Mount Hood, etched in pink by the setting sun. A cedar-shake house sat on the lip of the ridge, a deck curving out over the abrupt drop. The view was spectacular.

Their guides waited with obvious impatience at the top of steps leading to a double door into the house. *Be it ever so humble*, Ashley thought with a touch of whimsy. The home would not have looked out of place nestled in the exclusive west hills of Portland.

The inside more than lived up to the promise of the outside. The entire east wall of the large area they entered was glass, so that Mount Hood appeared to be part of the room. Ashley drifted across the room full of lengthening shadows, mesmerized by the glowing mountain.

A voice from the gloom startled her and she spun around, a move that woke the baby.

"Glad you could make it this evening. I'm Virgil Tysinger." A trim man of medium height came toward them. The fading sunlight barely touched his face. He moved toward McCord with his right hand outstretched. McCord stood there staring at him without expression. Tysinger's arm dropped to his side.

McCord's voice sounded harsh after Tysinger's mellow tones. "Do you want to explain the purpose of this abduction?"

Tysinger winced. "Abduction? Good God, man, what did that idiot say to give you that idea?"

"I don't remember the exact phrases. But when two more of your men added their persuasion, I decided I'd rather not have my wife and son upset."

There he goes again. We're going to play this little melodrama out to its bitter end, it seems.

McCord continued. "I was alone when he came to my office and insisted that my wife was there somewhere. He also insisted that she be brought along. 'Abducted' pretty well describes that sort of behavior, wouldn't you say?" McCord stood with legs slightly apart, balanced on the balls of his feet, his hands resting at his waist. The word *formidable* flashed through Ashley's mind.

Tysinger attempted a laugh that didn't quite come off. "Don't be absurd. Perhaps he was a little overzealous in making my wishes known to you. I don't hire men for their gifts of perception and subtlety." He leaned over and turned on a lamp sitting on a small table. "But you see, Raul, I could never reach you by phone, you never would return my calls, and it was important that I speak with you before you left town today. Really important.'' The smile on his face did not reach his dark eyes. They were wary, watching for a reaction.

McCord's smile wasn't pleasant. ''Then you've wasted your time and ours, Tysinger. I'm not Raul.''

Tysinger gave a start. ''You aren't Raul McCord?'' He glanced from McCord to Ashley, then back to McCord, and smiled. ''Nice try, McCord. I almost believed you, but you've been described to me.'' Tysinger wasn't as comfortable as he wanted them to believe. Ashley wondered if she would ever learn what was going on!

''What's that supposed to mean?'' McCord strolled to one end of the room, then turned to face Tysinger. ''Anyone fitting my general description has to be Raul? What's got you so uptight, Tysinger, that you start breaking some of the laws you've sworn to protect?''

Ashley watched the two men as they faced each other. Tysinger's uneasiness began to register on his face as he stared at the younger man. He seemed to take a firm grip on his temper, and his voice assumed a charming tone as he gestured to Ashley. ''I invited you and your wife here, McCord, to give us all a chance to get acquainted. I want to have the opportunity to sit down with both of you and discuss your activities these last few months.''

Activities? What were they supposed to have done?

"I admire your enthusiasm and your idealism, but I think you're a little misguided at the moment. I just don't want to see you rushing off with a bunch of misleading information that won't do anybody any good and could do a great deal of harm." He became more relaxed as his explanation proceeded. Ashley got the feeling that his speech had been rehearsed for just such an occasion.

"Mr. Tysinger." Ashley spoke for the first time since she'd entered the room. "I'm not quite sure how I got involved in this, but I have no idea what it's all about." She gave him her most winning smile. "I don't even know Mr. McCord. I just want to go home."

Tysinger listened to her with astonishment. When she finished he looked at McCord, then back at Ashley. "You're both good, I'll give you that. But then I already knew you were." *What was that supposed to mean?* "All right, so this is just a case of mistaken identity, is that it? Then who are you?" He waited for her response, a polite smile hovering at the edges of his thin lips.

Feeling more confident, Ashley introduced herself. "My name is Ashley Allison. I'm with the law firm of Begley, Henderson & Howe in Portland."

There was a flash of recognition on Tysinger's face; then it was gone. "Begley, Henderson & Howe. That's very interesting, Ms. Allison. You say you don't know Mr. McCord."

She glanced over at McCord, whose intent expression indicated that he was most interested in her answer. She shook her head. "No. I've never seen him before today."

"Tell me, Ms. Allison," Tysinger asked in a satin tone, "do you usually take a baby to work with you?" His tone continued to be polite, but the smile became more of a sneer.

Ashley had gotten so accustomed to holding the baby in her arms that she'd momentarily forgotten him. She glanced down as though astounded to find him there. "Oh. Well, you see, Mr. McCord handed him to me when I got on the elevator."

"Why did he do that, Ms. Allison?"

"I haven't the faintest idea."

Tysinger stared at McCord a moment. "Perhaps you can clarify all of this, McCord."

McCord glanced at Tysinger, then at Ashley. He was quiet as he looked at the baby, who watched him with wide-eyed wonder. Shaking his head, McCord assumed a grave expression. "My wife is still not fully recovered from Josh's birth. It was a very difficult time for her and the family has been doing what it can to help her." He walked over to Ashley and placed his arm about her shoulders. "This type of incident certainly doesn't help her to deal with everything. Her weakened physical state has created some emotional problems, but nothing that can't be overcome." He smiled down at her, the picture of loving concern.

At that moment, Ashley had no problem being the bewildered wife. Stunned would be a better description. Instead of explaining what sort of game he'd been playing, he'd taken the charade one step further. Not only was this man still insisting she was his wife, she had just discovered she was in delicate health. If she weren't so blasted tired at the moment she would have laughed. *Her* delicate? Her stamina had been the joke of the family for years.

Another lamp flicked on in the corner, drawing Ashley's attention away from the confrontation. She noticed a woman moving about the room, adjusting lights and shades. A rust carpet came into view, and the remaining walls, paneled in knotty pine, glinted in the lamplight.

Tysinger saw Ashley watching the other woman. "Pardon me, I neglected to introduce Mrs. Krueger. She and her husband live up here year 'round. They take care of the place for me." He turned to the other woman. "Mrs. Krueger, this is Mr. and Mrs. Mc-Cord and their young son." The woman nodded her head in silence. "Why don't you show Mrs. Mc-

Cord to the guest room? Perhaps she would like to freshen up before dinner." Turning back to Ashley he continued, his charm back in place. "If there's anything you need for the baby, I'm sure Mrs. Krueger will be able to help you. She's raised several of her own."

Ashley followed Mrs. Krueger out of the room, down a short hallway and into a large bedroom that also had a glass wall on its east side. *I'll bet the sunrises are spectacular in this place.*

Mrs. Krueger gestured to a door on the other side of a large bed. "There's a private bath attached to this room. Mr. Tysinger's room has one too, and my husband and I have our own apartment downstairs."

Puzzled, Ashley asked, "Downstairs? I thought this was a single-level house."

Mrs. Krueger's eyes crinkled mischievously, giving her face a gamine appearance. "Oh, no," she said. "This place is built along the side of a ridge and goes down two stories on the east side. We like it. It gives us our privacy when Mr. Tysinger entertains guests."

Mrs. Krueger smiled with obvious pleasure at the baby watching her from the security of Ashley's shoulder. "Would you like me to take your bright-eyed young man? He hasn't taken his eyes off me since we came in here." She stroked beneath Josh's chin so that he gave a quick kick that almost caused Ashley to drop him. She wasn't used to his sudden movements.

Mrs. Krueger asked a natural question that sent Ashley into a panic. "How old is he?"

Ashley gazed at her, trying to decide how to answer. Should she be coy and ask, "How old do you think he is?" or try to guess? For the first time since she'd laid eyes on him, Ashley was glad to see McCord walk into the room. The lopsided grin acknowledged Ashley's dilemma as he commented, "He'll be four months old next week, won't he, love?"

Ashley took her cue and tried to sound calm. "That's right."

Suddenly shy, Mrs. Krueger hastened to the door. "Dinner will be ready in about fifteen minutes. If you'd like, I could feed the baby in the kitchen while you eat."

Still unsure of herself in this area, Ashley looked to McCord for the proper answer.

"That would be a big help, Mrs. Krueger. Thank you. His bottles and food are all in the case I left in the other room."

Ashley handed Josh to Mrs. Krueger and watched as he left with yet another new person. *He has no sense of discrimination, but it's just as well. What would I have done on this trip if he'd cried the entire time?* It didn't bear thinking about.

The door closed. For the first time since McCord and Ashley had met at the elevator hours ago, they were alone.

Silence stretched between them like a rubber band waiting to be released. They watched each other warily, more than the width of the room dividing them.

"I'm sorry." McCord's voice carried to Ashley in firm tones.

She continued to watch him without expression. "Just what does that mean, Mr. McCord? Are you apologizing for your atrocious behavior or just making a general statement regarding your character?"

She could tell he didn't care much for her comment, but that was all right. Ashley didn't care much for anything about him at the moment. She'd had a rough day and, thanks to him, relief was several hours away.

He moved closer, then paused. He ran his hand through his hair, causing the waves to part into a cluster of curls on his forehead. They failed to soften the tight contours of his face. Now that she thought about it, he didn't appear to have gotten much rest lately either.

"Look, Ms. Allison, you have every right to be angry." He ignored her nod of agreement. "I understand that. Believe it or not, I had no idea this plan of mine would go so far." He swung away from her, no longer able to look at the closed expression on her face. "I needed a wife to fill in just for a few minutes, or so I thought at the time. The deception wasn't going to harm anyone, and it might have helped others." He glanced over his shoulder. She hadn't moved from her position near the door. He spun around, covering the distance between them in long strides. "I'm trying to buy time for some people, Ms. Allison. By pretending to be married, you and I are assisting others who've gone to a great deal of effort and taken serious risks to obtain information. This weekend they're trying to get the information into the right hands." He wanted so much to get her to understand the importance of what was happening, but it was too complicated to explain in a few short sentences. His frustration mounted.

"I'd been stalling Wilson, trying to come up with a story, when I saw you at the elevators this evening. I made an instant decision to use your presence to help me get out of a tight spot."

She stared at him in amazement. "If you feel that getting us both abducted is getting out of a tight spot, I'm not sure I want to know what you *consider* a tight spot."

McCord's hand raked through his already mussed hair. Then he rubbed the back of his neck and let out his breath in a heavy sigh. "You're right. I didn't handle this at all well. The hell of it is that I made the biggest sales pitch of my entire career in order to talk Jeanine into leaving Josh with me. She's never gone off and left him for more than a couple of hours before." Then, as though talking more to himself than to her, he continued. "Of course, if Josh hadn't been there, it wouldn't have occurred to me to try to impersonate anyone."

She ignored his last comment to latch on to the name he'd mentioned. "Jeanine?"

"Josh's mother."

"Of course, Josh's mother. Silly of me to forget."

"It made a lot more sense for him to stay here rather than to travel with her to Washington, D.C. Who could have guessed Tysinger would go to this extreme?"

"You do realize I haven't a solitary clue as to what you're talking about. I feel like Alice attempting a conversation with the Mad Hatter."

McCord stopped pacing and stared at her as though noticing her mood for the first time. "Most women I know would have had hysterics today." He tilted his head slightly as he studied her calm demeanor. "Why haven't you been screaming and hurling accusations?'' The more he thought about it, the more impressed he was with her self-control.

''It's rather trite to state the obvious. I'm not 'most women,' and my training helps me to disguise what I'm feeling.'' Her tone became more gentle. ''Of course, if you prefer hysteria and screaming, it won't take much for me to oblige you.''

His quick grin disappeared as he hastened to reassure her. ''No. No, thanks. I guess what I'm trying to do is to thank you for not continuing to protest to Tysinger. You lent credibility to my story, and I want you to know how very much I appreciate it.''

''Don't mention it,'' she replied in a disgusted tone. ''I felt like an absolute fool standing there denying that I knew either one of you while I clutched your baby in my arms.''

This time McCord's smile stayed in place. His hand rested lightly along her jawline as he peered down into her face. ''I'll admit to counting on that when I placed him in your arms. That, and the element of surprise. I planned to use you only to get out of the building and away from Wilson.'' His hand slid to the back of her neck, under the long hair, and gripped. ''What I wasn't counting on were the reinforcements that were used to get us into that car.'' His hand began to massage the tight muscles in her neck. ''That's when I realized I had miscalculated, and I got angry—at myself, at Tysinger, and at the situation I'd placed us in. Quite frankly, I'm not sure how we're going to get out of it, either.''

Ashley noticed the tired lines in his face. He wasn't the first person to make an impulsive decision that backfired, and there was certainly no point in her continuing to do battle with him. His long fingers were ridding her neck muscles of the stiffness caused by the long ride and the anxiety of wondering what was happening.

McCord interpreted her silence as unforgiving. Why not? Why should she forgive him for being such an idiot? She probably had a family waiting at home, frantic with worry.

"Your parents must be worried sick by now. Perhaps we can call them. I can tell Tysinger that we were supposed to be having dinner with them. Surely he'll understand that this trip wasn't in our plans?"

Her parents? How old did he think she was? "I don't live with my parents, Mr. McCord."

"Rafe."

"What?"

Dark red began to seep into his face. "I'm sorry, I've never bothered to introduce myself. I'm Raphael McCord. My friends call me Rafe."

Bewilderment flashed across her face. "Who is Raul?"

"My brother."

She backed away, leaning against the door. "Somehow that doesn't clarify much for me." She held up her palm. "But I don't think I'm capable of listening to many more of your 'explanations' tonight." A slight smile hovered around her mouth, and he could sense that her mood had lightened somewhat. He was surprised at his relief. For whatever obscure reason, he didn't want this woman to stay angry with him.

He smiled. "Well, is there someone who will be upset when you're late getting home tonight?" He wondered why he cared.

She wondered why he asked. "Just my roommate. But we don't always check in with each other." She mentally apologized to Tasha for that little lie. She just wished she *could* call her to explain and perhaps prevent the destruction of her home.

He gave her a searching look, trying to understand the expression on her face. "Well, if you'd like, we can contact your roommate."

Ashley didn't care for the emphasis on the word *roommate.* What did he want to know? Whether she was involved with someone? What about him? His wife hadn't been gone very long and he was pretending to be married to someone else. Her eyes took in the picture before her. A well-developed specimen of virile manhood, convinced, no doubt, that he could have any woman he wanted, turning on the charm for her. Her encounters with the opposite sex through the years had educated her about his type of male. Well, she didn't need any of them—this one, especially.

She walked past him, moving over to watch the fading colors reflected off the snow of Mount Hood. It was almost dark. "No, I don't think I'll call my roommate. She's Oriental and not accustomed to some of our Western ways." She glanced over her shoulders at him. "She's going to be upset, but there's not much I can do about it." And that's the truth, Ashley thought with a sigh.

Once again the room was quiet, but something had happened in the past few minutes. Their awareness of each other caused a strong pull between them. Ashley refused to acknowledge the attraction. Not only was she not interested in developing a relationship with any man, she found this particular man despicable. Her disgust with amorous married males knew no bounds.

Rafe watched her straight back and wondered what he'd said or done to cause the stiffening in her manner. For a few moments she had seemed to relax somewhat. Women! There was no understanding them, and at thirty-five, he no longer made the attempt. He shrugged his shoulders. They'd have dinner with Tysinger, listen to his political propositions, then ask to be excused. He didn't want to spend any more time around this prickly female than he had to.

"Guess we'd better find Tysinger, then, and get this meal behind us." His sudden comment sliced through the silence between them, causing her to start. Her control wasn't as complete as she would have liked it to be.

She turned and, with something of an effort, forced herself to give him a polite, meaningless smile. "You're right. The sooner we eat, the sooner we return to town."

Chapter Three

Ashley shifted, burying her face in the pillow. Her internal timepiece assured her that it was Saturday and she could enjoy a few moments extra in bed. She'd slept better than she had for weeks. Smiling with contentment, she stretched her full length, tightening each and every muscle just for the pleasure of relaxing afterwards. Maybe she'd run that morning. She'd missed doing that the last several mornings. At the moment, Ashley felt that all was right with her world.

"Do you intend to stay in bed all day?" a polite male voice inquired in her ear.

Ashley's eyes flew open. Silver blue eyes faced her from the adjoining pillow.

In an abrupt movement, Ashley sat up, staring around the room with bewilderment. *Where am I?* She saw Josh on a pile of blankets nearby, waving his hands and watching his fingers.

"Josh?"

"Yep, ole Josh and I have been up for hours. You must really sleep soundly to have missed all our activities this morning." Rafe watched her as their respective positions sifted through her morning fog. In a conversational tone he added, "I managed to bathe and feed him, so he seemed content to rest for a while." He watched the look of horror grow on her face and smiled. "I've been taking it easy, waiting for you to wake up."

Ashley groaned. She wrapped her arms around her knees and rested her head on them. Events of the night before began to filter through her memory. "I'm supposed to be married."

Rafe's hand moved up the length of her back, from hips to shoulders, as he massaged the muscles along her spine. The silkiness of her slip caused a tingling everywhere he touched.

"Would you stop that!" She jerked away from him. "I distinctly remember explaining to you that I was not going to share a bed with you last night. What are you doing here?"

Rafe folded his arms behind his head and smiled. "I got cold. At these heights the nights are always cold, and Josh seemed to have the spare blankets in this room. After the noise I made looking for blankets in the closet and all the drawers I began to realize that nothing would disturb you.'' His arm slipped from behind his head and gestured. ''As you can see, I was right. I crawled in and you never noticed.''

Ashley shook her head in a flurry of waves as her soft hair settled back around her shoulders. She refused to look at him.

In a judicious tone Rafe added, ''Something tells me you aren't a morning person.''

Exasperated with his cheerfulness, Ashley grabbed her pillow and placed it on her knees, resting her head once again. ''What was your first clue?'' Her muffled voice drifted to him. She scarcely recalled going to bed the night before. The events of the day had succeeded in knocking her out as effectively as a narcotic.

Still buried in her pillow, she tried to be fair. After all, it wasn't as though there wasn't enough room for two. The bed was large enough to use for a football scrimmage. On second thought, perhaps it would be better utilized for naval maneuvers. Her recent moves had caused a gentle, undulating movement across the expanse of satin comforter. Ashley would never have considered sleeping in a water bed. She tended to get seasick crossing the Willamette River on the Ross Island Bridge.

"It doesn't slosh," she mumbled.

"It's baffled."

Unaware that she'd spoken her thought out loud, Ashley was puzzled by his remark. She raised her head and looked over at him; he was sprawled propped up against the headboard. "What did you say?"

"The bed has baffles built in to lessen the wave action."

"Oh."

"Do I take it then that you had a restful night, all things considered?"

She eyed his bland expression with suspicion. "All of *what* things considered?"

"Oh, my getting up with Josh a couple of times and cuddling to keep you warm."

"You did what?" That woke her up. "There's no way I could have slept through that," she stated in emphatic tones.

"Whatever you say, dear. I don't want to start an argument before breakfast." Rafe appeared to have a problem holding his innocent expression.

"If I'd known you were the kind of person who goes back on his word, I would have insisted that you sleep in the other room."

His eyes danced in the morning sunlight, and it was hard for Ashley to ignore the mischief in them. "There are only two bedrooms on this floor and our host is using one of them." The reasonableness of his tone further incensed Ashley. "How could I explain that my wife expected me to sleep with the host? Are you trying to destroy my reputation?"

"Isn't that exactly what you're trying to do to mine?" she snapped back. "You're enjoying this, aren't you?" she demanded.

"I could be...very much." Rafe's voice held a velvety warmth and his hand once more slid up the length of her back.

Ashley's body reacted to the caress as though independent of her. Her anger was directed as much at herself as it was at him. "Isn't one wife enough for you, or do you get some kind of pleasure out of collecting women for the weekend under false pretenses?" Everywhere his hand touched, tiny electrical impulses shot through her skin, causing it to tingle.

Rafe spoke in a confidential tone. "I wonder if Tysinger's recovered from the verbal attack you launched when he insisted that we take advantage of his hospitality and spend the weekend."

Ashley conceded, "Well, I suppose I could have been a little more tactful."

At that Rafe began to laugh.

"I'd barely accepted the idea of filling in as your wife through dinner when he suggested an overnight stay. That was too much."

"So you told him last night. I thought your threatening to have him arrested for kidnapping added a nice touch to the dinner conversation."

"And don't think I won't, just as soon as I can get away from this place. And why weren't *you* protesting when he insisted we stay here?"

"You were doing such an excellent job of it, I felt that anything I could have added would have been redundant. Besides, I have Tysinger's full sympathy and grudging respect for tolerating a wife with a temper like yours."

"I am not your wife," Ashley stated through clenched teeth. "Please stop calling me that." Rafe's feathery caresses caused her blood to quicken as warmth began to flow through her body.

Still grinning, Rafe added, "Confiding to Tysinger that you didn't have any idea who fathered Josh certainly has him speculating on your morals."

"*My* morals! I don't go around claiming marriage ties to every stranger I meet."

"Neither do I. You happen to be the first." Changing the subject, Rafe continued. "Don't you think it's time we got out of bed?" he queried. Had he no notion of what his hand was doing to her? Apparently not, and for that small blessing she gave thanks. She kept her flushed face resolutely turned away from him.

"Yes, I would be delighted to get up, get dressed, and go home!" Ashley felt a sudden, soft movement of the bed and glanced around in time to see Rafe as he threw back the covers and stood up. She got a quick glimpse of a great expanse of dark flesh. Averting her head, she asked, "Would you mind getting out of here so I can get dressed?"

"Isn't it a little late for modesty after sleeping with me all night?" Her pillow hit the bathroom door just as he closed it behind him. She could hear his laughter.

Never had anyone dared to treat Ashley in this manner. She'd never have stood for it. But what choice did she have at the moment? Why wasn't Jeanine here where she was supposed to be? And why had she disappeared to Washington, D.C.? The mystery was beginning to bother Ashley more the longer she thought about it. She was determined to get some answers to her questions that day. She deserved that much after his disruption in her life.

Ashley came out of the shower much refreshed and ready to face the day. She picked up the wilted cream blouse she'd worn the day before just as the bedroom door swung open.

"Can't you knock?" She clutched at the large bath towel wrapped around her and glared at Rafe as he sauntered into the room.

"I suppose I could, but frankly, I didn't give it much thought. Mrs. Krueger felt sorry for you having to hobble around in your high heels and suggested that you try on some of her younger son's clothes." He handed her a bundle of clothing. "She said he left these the last time he was here."

She shook out a pair of well-worn jeans and decided that they would do nicely. A pair of sneakers appeared to be about her size. With as much dignity as possible, given that only her towel stood between modesty and embarrassment, Ashley gathered up a pullover knit shirt and the jeans and sneakers and stalked back into the bathroom.

The navy and white striped shirt clung to her curves. Ashley frowned into the mirror, then shrugged her shoulders. It couldn't be helped. The jeans were snug but the length was right. Once again she had cause to be thankful for long legs. Now she was ready to face the world and do battle, if necessary.

Ashley studied the bathroom, still unused to the luxury of her surroundings. Had she given much thought to the idea, she would have imagined that kidnap victims would be forced to endure privation and severe discomfort, not to mention starvation. If the previous night's meal was any indication, severe dieting would be a necessity after a lengthy captivity around Mrs. Krueger.

Ashley faced an empty bedroom when she came out of the bathroom, and she set off in search of her new family.

She heard Tysinger's voice and halted. "I realize you young people plan to save the world, and I admire that. Why, I'm well known for my interest in the environment and the preservation of our natural resources." Ashley stepped to the door of the living room. Tysinger paced in front of the fireplace as Rafe sat on the sofa bouncing Josh in a gentle rhythm on his knee. "I'm not against what you're doing and what you stand for. I want you to understand that. I admire you tremendously." Ashley's movement at the door caught the pacing man's notice and he stopped abruptly. She walked into the room, her eyes trained on Tysinger's face.

"Good morning." She stopped behind the sofa, her hand resting lightly upon Rafe's shoulder. Rafe reached up and pulled her hand against his cheek. *We can't look any more domestic than this,* she thought. She was weary of the role playing, regardless of how helpful it was supposed to be to Rafe. She just wanted to go home.

Tysinger stared at her with a hint of surprise and she acknowledged to herself that her casual outfit gave an entirely different impression from the business attire of the evening before. "Good morning, Mrs. McCord. I trust you spent a pleasant night."

She stared back at him. "Yes, Mr. Tysinger, I did. However, I do want you to understand that I don't intend to stay here any longer. I didn't appreciate your high-handed attitude last night, but you got your way. Hopefully, that's satisfied whatever quirk caused you to drag us up here in the first place."

Tysinger's glance veered to Rafe with what could have been sympathy in his eyes. "As I attempted to explain last night, Mrs. McCord, I've been trying for some time to meet with you and your husband and discuss his recent activities. The matter was too important to postpone any longer. I thought I made that quite plain."

What was the use in trying to make him understand that she wasn't Mrs. McCord? And did she even want to at this point? After all, she'd just spent the night with the man. Ashley attempted a smile. "Well, then, why don't I leave you two men to discuss whatever, and I'll just get back to town." She smiled down at the top of Rafe's head in what she hoped was a wifely expression of encouragement.

As Rafe moved to stand up, Tysinger exploded his next little bombshell. "Unfortunately, I'm a little short on transportation at the moment, Mrs. Mc-Cord. Mrs. Krueger sent for some supplies, and I'm not sure when the car will be returning."

"Well, then, call a cab or something," Ashley suggested, trying to hang on to her hard-won composure. "I can't believe we're just stranded up here."

A wary smile appeared as Tysinger explained. "I don't have phone service up here. I don't want to be bothered by all the so-called emergency interruptions when I manage to get away." Rafe walked around the sofa and placed his hand at Ashley's waist. He had a pretty good idea how she was taking this latest piece of news. Tysinger continued. "I sincerely thought you and your husband would enjoy being up here."

The man was incredible, Ashley thought with amazement. He actually looked and sounded offended. The stage had lost out when he chose politics.

Rafe pulled her closer to him. "Tysinger mentioned that some of the trails around here have spectacular views. He thought we might want to go for a walk—enjoy the sunshine and get a little exercise." He squeezed her waist as she looked up at him. "Perhaps by the time we get back, the car will be here and we can get back to town." Glancing back at Tysinger, Rafe continued. "My wife still gets upset rather easily. You have my word that we won't be flying East if you'll get us back to Portland."

The two men stood there in silent communication. Then Tysinger smiled. "Fine, McCord. I knew you'd see things a little more clearly if I just had a chance to discuss them with you. The car should be back in a couple of hours, so why don't you take that walk you mentioned? I know you'll both enjoy it.'' He left the room with a definite bounce to his step.

Ashley noticed that the baby in Rafe's arms had fallen asleep. ''What about Josh? We can't just go off and leave him.''

''I suppose we could, but I don't intend to. I'll take him with us, but let's get you some coffee and a piece of Mrs. Krueger's coffee cake. You'll need strength for that hike.'' He took her by the hand and led her into the kitchen.

Rafe was right, she decided as she viewed the glistening day from the kitchen window. She might as well relax and enjoy the next few hours, since there was little else she could do.

After a generous helping of coffee cake and several cups of coffee, Ashley felt ready to hike back to town, but decided she might be a little overambitious. She went looking for Rafe and found him dressing the baby for the outdoors. When Josh saw her he gave her one of his exuberant smiles.

''What a flirt you are. Almost as bad as your father.''

Rafe ignored her comment. Not that he didn't deserve it, she decided some time later as she set off behind him on one of the trails. However, she couldn't fault him as a father. Rafe appeared familiar with Josh's routine and made sure all his needs were met.

In the serenity of the mountain forest, Ashley began to relax. The scent of cedar pleased her. Whenever she smelled cedar she thought of her mother and her treasured mementos stored in an old cedar chest.

A ground squirrel caught her eye, and she stopped to watch his antics as he flitted around, then paused to scold her. Somehow she lost track of Rafe. When she glanced back at the trail he was no longer in sight. She stopped, concerned; the trail branched off and she was unsure which direction he'd taken. Eventually she chose to follow the trail going downward, hoping he'd opted for the same one. Ashley had no desire to try to find her way out of there on her own. She quickened her steps in hopes of catching up with him.

The trail made a sharp turn, and Ashley gave a quick sigh of relief. Rafe stood on a ledge overlooking the lake. The sun had burned off the early morning haze and left the air clear. A windfall tree, no doubt a casualty of the winter, lay alongside the trail. Rafe sat down and propped Josh up against him. Josh found his favorite fingers and enjoyed the view from the security of Rafe's arms.

Ashley noticed that Rafe's shoes were not the handmade Italian leather shoes he'd worn the day before. "Where did you get your sneakers?"

He glanced down at his feet and smiled. "Tysinger had several pairs in his closet for 'drop-ins' and suggested that I make use of them. These aren't climbing shoes, but they beat the ones I wore yesterday."

Ashley had already noticed the snug-fitting jeans he wore with a yellow knit pullover shirt. The color enhanced his dark attractiveness.

She turned away from him to explore the edge of the bluff. The ground dropped about five feet to the edge of the water. She knelt at the edge and watched tiny fish feeding along the top of the water.

Rafe cleared his throat. "I thought if we could get away from Tysinger I'd try to fill you in on why Tysinger wants us here." He watched her as she peered over the side of the ledge, her profile defined by the thick shrubs bordering the path.

She made a gentle correction. "Why Tysinger wants *you* here, not me."

"Actually, it isn't me he wants, it's Raul."

She turned to look at him, then back on her heels. "That's right. He called you Raul last night, didn't he? So he really wants your brother?"

"Yes, my brother and his wife Jeanine."

Her eyes widened. "You mean Jeanine is married to Raul, not to you?"

He was amused at her reaction. "That's correct. And Josh is their son. I'm just baby-sitting for the weekend."

She tried to sort through the confusion in her mind.

"I wanted you to understand that I wasn't trying to play some kind of game with you this morning. I'm not married."

She schooled her face to show no reaction to his news. "The whole story was sheer fabrication, wasn't it?"

He nodded. "As I explained last night, it wasn't one of my better ideas."

She shook her head in confusion. "Okay, so Tysinger thinks you and I are Raul and Jeanine, and he wanted to talk to them before they went to D.C." She looked up at him. "Do I understand so far?" She was more curious than angry at this point.

"Yes. Jeanine and Raul arranged to fly to Washington to meet with Senator Hensley this weekend. Tysinger made it obvious yesterday that he didn't want them to contact Hensley until he talked to them."

Ashley moved from her position on the ground and joined Rafe on the fallen log. "Where does Senator Hensley fit into all of this?"

"Raul and Jeanine became friends with W. A. Hensley when they helped with his campaign for the senate a few years ago. When they stumbled onto some unexpected information during a recent survey they were doing, Raul wasn't sure who to talk to about it. It touched several people involved in Oregon politics, and he decided to talk to someone he could trust."

Ashley waited for him to continue. She noticed Josh draped across Rafe's arm, fast asleep. When Rafe glanced down he smiled and placed the sleeping infant on his shoulder.

"Raul and Jeanine were helping a group of conservationists with a survey in southern Oregon designed to determine the effect of the herbicide sprays being used in that area."

"Now that's one controversy I've heard of. The media mentions it on a regular basis."

"I know. While in the midst of the survey, Raul and Jeanine discovered a group within the conservationist movement that had a strong reason to fight the use of herbicides. It killed their prolific crops of marijuana."

Ashley sat next to Rafe, contemplating the tranquil scene before them and trying to understand how the growing of marijuana in southern Oregon was responsible for her spending the weekend with Raphael McCord.

"Does Tysinger have something to do with the marijuana?" She watched the shifting leaves shadow Rafe's face as he admired the view.

"From his actions this weekend, I'm very much afraid that Tysinger is up to his neck in the mess. Otherwise, why would he take such drastic action to stop Raul and Jeanine from taking their information to Hensley?"

"Why would a politician jeopardize his career like that?"

Rafe stood up and began to follow the trail that paralleled the lake. Ashley wandered along beside him as he pondered her question. Eventually he shook his head. "I don't know. There could be several motives: greed, the desire for ever more power, who knows?" He paused as they reached a clearing and looked around. From this view they could see Tysinger's home perched on the ridge above them; the Kruegers' quarters were clearly visible. "Maybe he needs money to support some of his more expensive habits, such as his home up there."

"I wonder what Tysinger is going to do when he finds out that he didn't stop them from going to Washington."

Rafe's eyes reminded Ashley of arctic glaciers as he continued to stare at the house on the ridge. "That's what concerns me at the moment. Why don't we head back? The car should have returned by now, and I'd prefer to be away from here when Ty-singer gets that piece of news.''

''Do you think he's going to let us go?''

''He's an intelligent man. If he's thinking at all, he knows he can't keep us.'' He put his arm around her shoulders and pulled her toward him. ''I can't get too angry at the man. Because of his little plot, I had this chance to meet you.''

Ashley started at the personal turn of the conversation. Why had she thought his eyes looked cold? At the moment, the warm regard in his eyes caused a definite skip in her steady pulse. His lips touched hers with gentle pressure, giving her the opportunity to pull away. She had no intention of getting involved with this man, but inertia seemed to have set in. It was far easier to stay in the circle of his arm. As he felt her relax, his arm tightened, pulling her hard against his chest. Her hand came up to rest against Josh's back as he lay curled on Rafe's shoulder. Somehow it felt right to be in the circle of his arms with the baby. Rafe deepened the kiss and Ashley could no longer think. His gentle insistence as he explored her soft lips affected her more deeply than a passionate kiss could have done. This man was rapidly reaching a part of Ashley that she had never known existed, and she wasn't at all sure she could handle the emotions he was provoking.

Chapter Four

Their return to Tysinger's home took place in silence. Mrs. Krueger met them at the door. "Why don't I take this young man and let you enjoy some time alone together?" She took the slumbering baby from Rafe's shoulder with a smile. "My supplies arrived. I ordered more baby food to be on the safe side. I also had them bring more disposable diapers. That's something they didn't have when I was raising mine, and I have to admit they're convenient."

Ashley followed Mrs. Krueger into the house. "You shouldn't have gone to so much trouble, Mrs. Krueger. Now that the car is back, we'll be leaving."

Mrs. Krueger turned a puzzled face to Rafe and Ashley. "I didn't realize you planned to leave so soon. Mr. Tysinger must have forgotten. When the men came back they brought him a message that caused him to rush right out of here. He didn't say when he'd be back."

"They left?" Ashley repeated in disbelief. "But they couldn't have!"

"It looks as if we're stranded for a while, Ashley." Rafe's voice held a warning note in it.

Mrs. Kreuger nodded uncertainly. "Let me put this little fella down. Lunch is ready whenever you are." She disappeared with Josh.

Ashley whirled to face Rafe. "Do you think they learned something about Raul and Jeanine?"

Rafe seemed to ignore the urgent question for a moment; then he spoke. "It's a possibility. I don't particularly want to face him if that's the news." He crossed to the front door and stepped through, eyeing the trail they'd taken the day before.

"Is there any way we can follow that trail back down to the highway?" Ashley peered around his shoulder.

Rafe's hands rested on his slim hips as he stared out over the thousands of acres around them, the dense forest covering the mountains with a mantle of green velvet.

"I probably could, but not with you and Josh along." He turned to her and noticed her expression. "Look, I don't intend to go anywhere and leave you and Josh, so quit looking at me like that. I got you into this mess and I intend to get you out." He leaned against the rail for a few moments in deep thought.

Mrs. Kreuger appeared at the door. "I have lunch set up for you on the deck. The weather's too nice to waste inside." Ashley responded to her thoughtfulness with a smile, then turned to Rafe.

"Let's get something to eat. This mountain air has made me ravenous—you'll think of something." She heard her reassurance with some astonishment. *She* had no idea what to do, so why did she feel confident he'd find a solution? It was certainly out of character for Ashley to rely on anyone but herself.

They ate lunch in silence. Ashley's few attempts at conversation were answered with absentminded replies, and she soon gave up. Besides, when had she ever had a better opportunity to enjoy the Cascade Mountains? When she moved to Oregon one of her first plans had been to join a hiking club and enjoy the outdoors that were such a contrast to the ranch she had called home. Instead she became absorbed in trial work and the weeks, months, and eventually years slipped away unnoticed as she began to make a name for herself in the legal field. She learned to accept that a woman in the profession had to work twice as hard as a man, in order to prove herself capable.

Watching the silent Rafe methodically eat his fresh fruit salad and man-size sandwich, Ashley recognized with some surprise that she'd spent more consecutive time with this man than she'd spent with any man since she had left Texas. She had dated occasionally at first, but then found she didn't have time even for that. She had given up dating with no regret. She could not ask for more from life than to pursue the career that fulfilled and sustained her.

Early in her life, Ashley had come to believe that love for a man became a sort of bondage for a woman. Her father and her four older brothers had run the family cattle ranch and, while there was no doubt in Ashley's mind that her dad loved her mother dearly, he gave no thought to the countless demands ranch life made on her, trying to keep five hungry males fed and clothed and cared for. Ashley grew up with the belief that love and marriage, for a woman, meant never having any time for herself and her own needs.

The piano had always been her mother's escape, but Ashley was in her teens before she discovered that her mother had been offered a scholarship to the Fort Worth Conservatory of Music. Ashley's father, afraid he would lose her mother if she went away to school, had convinced her to marry him instead of going to the conservatory. When Ashley learned of this, she decided that *she* would never make that mistake. She had her mother's support when she decided to study law. Marriage would never hold any appeal for Ashley.

"What a ferocious expression you have on your face." Rafe must have been watching her for some time. She flushed with embarrassment.

"Well, did you come up with a solution in all of this quiet?" She hoped her change of subject would allow her to avoid having to explain her thoughts.

"I guess I've been thinking more about what Tysinger is going to do when he finds out this visit didn't accomplish what he'd hoped it would."

"He'd better not try anything else. He's already in enough trouble because of kidnapping us. That's certainly not going to increase his political popularity."

"In the first place, he's going to deny any accusation of kidnapping; he made that clear last night. His story is going to be that it was all a misunderstanding, and how do we disprove that? Have we been threatened, mistreated, abandoned? We're going to look foolish accusing him of forcing us to have a luxurious and secluded weekend together in the mountains."

Ashley began to laugh at the word picture Rafe painted. "You know, I'll bet that's exactly what he'll say. Can't you just hear him now? Here he has Mrs. Krueger busy taking care of us and preparing her

scrumptious meals, and we sit plotting ways to escape. The whole thing's a farce.''

''That's what I've been thinking. Another is, how
long do we have before we *must* get back. I presume
you need to be at work on Monday.'' She nodded in
agreement. ''I have to be back in San Francisco for
a ten o'clock appointment on Monday.'' She looked
startled and he stopped. ''What's wrong?''

''You don't live in Oregon?''

''No. Most of my business interests are located in
California. Raul opened the plastics plant here in
Oregon a few years ago, but I have no connection
with it.''

She began to smile. ''For a man with whom I've
spent almost twenty-four hours of uninterrupted
time, you're still very much a mystery to me.'' Her
eyes lit with humor and caught Rafe's attention. He
lost the thread of their conversation as he admired
her animated face. With reluctance he forced his
mind back to what they had been saying.

''You're as much a mystery to me. We haven't had
much time to get acquainted, but we can always
remedy that, you know.'' She didn't trust the gleam
that appeared in his eyes.

''That's all right.'' She refused to meet his eyes.
''We probably won't ever see each other after this
weekend.''

He reached over and took her hand, waiting until she raised her eyes to meet his. "Ashley, I come up to visit Raul and Jeanine frequently. There's no reason why you and I shouldn't see each other, is there?"

He wanted to know whether she was involved with someone else. If only it were that simple. "I'm pretty well tied up with my practice, Rafe. I don't have much time for socializing."

"Your practice?" Her statement disconcerted him; she could tell by his startled expression.

"I told you last night that I'm an attorney. At least, I told Tysinger."

He sat there staring at her as though she'd whipped out a baseball bat and thumped him over the head.

"You're a lawyer?" he repeated, convinced he'd misunderstood.

She nodded. "Yes, I'm with the law firm of Begley, Henderson & Howe." Why did he seem so shocked?

His next question surprised her. "How old are you, anyway?"

"Twenty-eight. Why?"

He leaned back in his chair, his hands resting on the table, and shook his head. "I feel like a complete fool," he admitted with a shrug. "I thought you were a college student working during the summer. I didn't think you were more than twenty-one years old."

"Thank you very much, I think. I wondered what made you think I lived with my parents, but it never dawned on me that you didn't understand I've got a law practice."

"Wouldn't you know," he muttered.

She could feel tension begin to tickle her neck like hackles rising on a dog. "What do you mean?" Once again she felt defensive about her choice of career.

Rafe gave her a rueful grin. "Nothing, really. Lawyers don't happen to be my favorite brand of people, and it never occurred to me that you were one of them." His grin broadened. "Now that I think about it, your attack on Tysinger last night was more in the way of a professional performance. I guess I should have realized that at the time."

"What do you have against lawyers?"

"I don't think the majority of them have enough business sense to set themselves up as soothsayers, but that hasn't stopped them as far as my business is concerned. They're an unmitigated nuisance to have around, but a necessary evil."

"What exactly is your business, Mr. McCord?" She found his amusement offensive.

"I buy into ailing companies and try to turn them into profitable businesses. Many times a business will fail because legal advisors are allowed to make business decisions."

"I take it that you've made the right decisions and saved your ailing companies."

"Most of them."

"A real knight in shining armor, is that right?" Her sarcasm touched a nerve: his jaw clenched as he stared at her.

"Obviously, I'm not *your* knight unless I can come up with a way to rescue you from your dragon—Tysinger." He pushed back his chair and stood up. "If you'll excuse me."

Ashley sat at the table long after she heard the front door close behind Rafe. Why had she baited him like that? He'd shown her nothing but courtesy and kindness since she'd met him. Why did she feel the need to ridicule him? Her behavior since she had met Rafe continued to confuse her.

Hours later, Ashley sat once again on the deck, waiting for Rafe to reappear. Patience had never been one of her virtues. She'd had plenty of time to review the events leading up to his disappearance and had even framed several apologies during the three hours he'd been gone.

She'd finally faced the fact that her reaction to Raphael McCord was more violent than any she'd experienced in the past. His sudden appearance anywhere around her set her nerves on edge, but why couldn't she at least be polite to him, even if friendliness seemed to be beyond her? Her puzzling seesaw of emotions was causing her a great deal of distress. She hated to admit to herself that her usual friendly and outgoing disposition had gone into hibernation during the past two days. If she didn't watch it she'd turn into a crochety caricature of spinsterhood.

She blamed part of her confusion on the romantic surroundings of the Mount Hood National Forest in the summertime. It was easy to forget the real world and bask in the lazy warmth of the sunshine. Ashley had spent the earlier part of the afternoon getting acquainted with Josh. She'd found him quite amazing and wondered whether all babies were so smart. He'd spotted her good-luck pendant, which hung from a gold chain at her throat, and managed to grab it as it swung past his waving arms. His tenacious grip caused quite a tussle before she managed to free herself without hurting him.

Ashley admitted to herself that she was enjoying her acquaintance with Josh, which surprised her. She wasn't a domesticated woman. Perhaps an unconscious desire to escape the role of her mother had caused the younger Ashley to refuse to learn the housewifely arts. As a result she could neither cook nor sew.

She was satisfied with her life and would never have given the matter a thought if she hadn't met Raphael McCord. She jumped up and walked over to the railing. There was no reason to let him upset her life any more than he'd already done.

The lake looked inviting, but even if she'd had a swimsuit she wouldn't have gone in; she knew the water was close to freezing. Melting snow kept the lake at a high level. As she stood there admiring the scenery she heard whistling down below.

Leaning over the railing, Ashley peered in the direction of the sound and saw Rafe move out of the trees. The sight of him caused her heart to lurch in her chest and she forgot to breathe.

He didn't see her watching him as he strode across the clearing, his movements like those of a big cat silently stalking. The memory of his kisses leaped into her mind. Ashley gave herself a shake, resenting her purely physical response to him. *I wonder if there's a pill to take to counteract my reactions?*

"Did you find a way out of here?" she called to get his attention. Rafe saw her and turned toward her. He stood below, hands resting on his hips, his chest moving visibly in his effort to breathe more easily in the thin air. His smile erased the earlier hostility between them.

"I think so. We can get away, but I'm not sure when."

Ashley gave no thought to why she felt relief that he was no longer angry. She returned his smile. "So what do we do?"

"Hang on. I've got to get cleaned up a bit. I must have hiked five miles since I last saw you." He looked over his shoulder at the lake and back at her. Then he waved and disappeared around the corner of the house.

Ashley started to dash back into the house but decided to show a little more dignity by strolling into the kitchen. Mrs. Krueger looked up from cutting salad vegetables and smiled. "How is your son?"

"Oh. I put him down after his bottle and he conked out in no time. He's probably awake by now—maybe I should check on him."

As she turned toward the hallway, Mrs. Krueger asked, "Is there anything in particular you would like to have for dinner?"

"Anything sounds fine to me so long as I don't have to make it. Cooking is not one of my skills."

Mrs. Krueger's face lit up with astonishment. "You mean you don't cook for Mr. McCord?"

I've done it again, she scolded herself. "Of course I cook for him, but I don't go to a lot of trouble." That didn't sound any better. "What I mean is, I, uh, I think I hear Josh." Ashley escaped down the hallway. In her need to make a hasty retreat she burst into the bedroom, where she came to an abrupt halt.

Rafe was walking out of the bathroom toweling his hair and wearing the smallest pair of briefs Ashley had ever seen. Her mouth dropped open.

"Don't you ever knock?" he asked in a fair imitation of her tone of voice earlier in the day.

She realized where she was staring and spun around toward Josh. "I thought I heard Josh."

"Obviously not, if our voices haven't disturbed him. You must have worn him out today."

She thought over her afternoon with Josh and grinned. When she heard the zip of Rafe's pants, Ashley figured he was decently covered and turned back around. His bare chest tugged at her attention, and she studied the thick mat of fur spread across it as though she'd be tested on it the next day. She managed to bring her eyes up to meet his and nodded, intent on concealing her reactions.

"Yes, Josh and I spent quite a time together. I've discovered that he loves to pull hair and is fascinated by my pendant. Do you realize he can move himself? He gets his knees under him, then lunges and scoots on his stomach." Rafe watched her as her eyes sparkled with the description.

"What color are your eyes?" he asked, interrupting her.

The change of subject surprised her, and she stood there for a moment in confusion. "My driver's license says blue. Why?"

"Because when I first saw you in the elevator they appeared to be gray. Today on our hike they were more of a jade green, and now they have a misty blue look about them." He walked to where she stood as though to examine them closer.

His proximity unnerved her. She wished he'd put on a shirt.

"My mom used to tease me about my eyes. She said they're like a mood ring."

Rafe pulled her to him and she looked up. The expression on his face caused her knees to turn to jelly. He lowered his head as he murmured, "What mood are you in at the moment?" His breath caressed her mouth as his lips touched hers in a tentative manner. Without thought Ashley relaxed in his arms and offered him her mouth, which he took with a sudden possession that seared through her. His mouth began to mold hers as his tongue touched her upper lip, then slipped into her mouth. She reached up to him, her arms sliding behind his head in an effort to get closer.

His hands moved along her back, continuing the exploration they had begun that morning, and discovered the indentation at her waist as well as the flare of her rounded hips. He pressed her body closer, showing her the effect she had on him.

Her hands had not been still. She brought them back to his chest and touched all the places her eyes had feasted upon earlier.

The sounds of Josh stirring from his nap began to seep into Ashley's consciousness, and she fought to regain control of herself. She managed to pull away from Rafe and opened her eyes. He looked at her hungrily, making no effort to hide his desire for her.

She turned away from him, struggling for composure. "What did you find out this afternoon?" she asked in an attempt to sound casual as she moved over to Josh and picked him up. She kept her head down as she sorted through the baby's clothing for something dry to put on him.

The amusement in Rafe's voice acknowledged the reason for her change of subject. "I found out that Tysinger isn't without communication here. He's got a short-wave unit somewhere, according to one of his neighbors." Rafe walked over and grabbed a fresh knit shirt from the bed, slipping it over his head. Ashley wondered where he kept getting all the shirts.

"You mean they have neighbors here?"

"Everyone has his own idea of what a neighbor is. I found a small cabin located on one of the tributaries that feeds into the Clackamas River." He sat down on the edge of the bed and pulled on his sneakers. "The man who lives there is probably in his late sixties. He was pleased to pass the time with me and share some of his fishing and hunting yarns." He watched her as she laid the baby down on the bed beside him. She refused to look at him as he continued. "He lives up here year 'round and said there are several families scattered around the area who stay in touch with each other to make sure everything is all right."

Ashley managed to change Josh's diaper and attempted a glance at Rafe as she picked up the baby. He was watching her intently and she could feel her color rise. In a lazy movement he stood up and placed his arms around her waist, Josh cuddled close between them. Ashley had trouble concentrating on his words.

"In the course of our conversation I asked how anyone managed to communicate with the outside world, and he told me about the Kruegers. He didn't know Tysinger's name and didn't seem all that interested in who I was, so I didn't bother to explain. The Kruegers seem to be well liked in the area and are known to be willing to help out whenever needed."

Ashley tried to withstand the heat of his stare as she asked, "Where is Mr. Krueger? I haven't seen anyone by that name, now that you mention it."

"I wondered the same thing. It seems that one of their sons is a logger and asked his dad to help with one of his rigs for a few weeks. He's been gone for a couple of weeks now. I was amazed at how much the man knew about what was going on with everyone." He paused, then added with a thoughtful expression, "He may already have known who I was, for that matter."

"You mean he may have thought you were Raul."

The mischievous grin Ashley found so attractive stole across Rafe's face. "Yes, I guess you're right. I never realized just how much I might enjoy playing house."

Her back stiffened. "I don't know what you have in mind, Rafe, but I don't intend to play house. Not with you—not with anyone."

She stepped away from his loose grasp and smiled. "You should wipe the lipstick off. Something tells me Mrs. Krueger might wonder why you're wearing that particular shade."

He grinned. "Do you really think so? For some reason I feel certain she'd understand exactly why I'm wearing it." He reached into a back pocket for his handkerchief.

Ashley was thankful that Josh was there at the moment. She needed some breathing space. One kiss and her knees gave way. For the first time in her life, Ashley began to appreciate how easy it would be to get carried away by a sensual response. She found it most irritating to discover a passionate nature behind her no-nonsense outlook on life. She consoled herself with the thought that the particular circumstances were far from normal, so she intended to ignore her reactions.

When she entered the living room, Ashley discovered that Mrs. Krueger had been busy. A small table containing two place settings and a flower centerpiece sat before the glass wall. A pair of candles shone in the early evening light.

"Mrs. Krueger, you're a magician. Everything is beautiful." Mrs. Krueger beamed her pleasure at Ashley's approval. "Aren't you going to join us?"

"Oh, no! This is your weekend to be alone and enjoy each other. If you don't mind, I'll take your young man and keep him entertained while the two of you enjoy some privacy."

That's all I need, Ashley thought in mounting frustration. *Everybody's determined to put us in a romantic setting.*

Rafe followed her into the room, and she waited for his comments. Instead, the room echoed with the unspoken thoughts and undercurrents Ashley had tried to leave in the bedroom. She shrugged and decided she might as well enjoy the evening.

She did. The dinner of broiled steaks, baked potatoes, and tossed salad was delicious. A light rosé wine glinted in the candlelight as they sipped from tulip glasses. They relaxed and chatted easily.

Rafe shared a little of his childhood. "Raul and I are less than two years apart in age and looked enough alike to be twins. Somehow we managed to keep our neighborhood in an uproar during our early years.''

''There were just the two of you in the family?''

''Yes, much to Mom's shame. She'd come from a large family and felt she hadn't done her part to re-populate the Ramirez family.''

''Ramirez?''

''My mother's family. She was a fourth-generation Californian. The family owns a fair amount of land in the north central part of the state.''

''McCord doesn't have much of a Spanish sound to it.''

''So I've been told. My father is of Scottish de-scent—and a quiet, introverted sort. He and Mom made quite a pair.'' He shook his head at some of his memories. ''Mom had a very fiery temperament, while Dad always tried to look at things from a rea-sonable, rational, logical viewpoint. When he and Mom had an argument he would give her all the nu-merous reasons why he was right and then fall apart when she broke down and cried. He loved her very much. We all did.''

Ashley watched his face gentle with memories from his past. She had trouble seeing him as a little boy—he must have been a handful.

Rafe glanced up and caught her smiling at him. He picked up his glass of wine, tipped it against hers, and said, "When do I get a chance to meet the Allison tribe? Will they give me a hard time because I want to run off with their only sister and daughter?"

The sudden change in subject, together with his careless remark, caused Ashley to choke on her wine. Trying to look and sound composed, she responded: "I'm afraid all of this is news to me. Has your role-playing gotten out of hand?"

"Not exactly. I suppose now that I've found you I don't intend to lose track of you." The smile that accompanied his statement did not lessen the seriousness of the expression in his eyes.

Ignoring the sudden increase in her pulse rate, Ashley spoke carefully. "I thought I made myself clear earlier. I don't have any serious relationships because I don't choose to have them."

"What makes you think I'm serious?" he retorted.

"Let me rephrase my remark. I'm not interested in having affairs. They only complicate matters, and someone always gets hurt." Her eyes glowed in the candlelight as she stared across the small table at him. "We're in a freakish situation this weekend; we've been thrown together under intimate circumstances that most newly acquainted people don't have to face."

"Are you referring to our impetuous marriage?"

"Our what?"

"Wouldn't you consider a marriage that took place as two people stepped into an elevator together rather impetuous?" His dancing eyes urged her to share his amusement in their predicament.

"I'd call it insanity. Whatever you label it, I'm not interested." She stood up from the table and took her wine glass into the shadows of the room. "So these elaborate scenes are being wasted, as far as I'm concerned."

He followed her and found her seated at the end of the sofa. He switched on a lamp as he sat at the other end. "Do you think I've set all this up as some sort of seduction scene?" His voice sounded almost angry.

"No, I don't think you've had to do anything but go along with Tysinger's plans. If we were married I could see what a nice weekend this would be. I'm sure Raul and Jeanine would have enjoyed it." Her tone stayed calm. Only she saw the slight tremor in her hand. When he made no comment she went on. "How do you propose to get us down from here?"

His eyes darted to hers in surprise. His mind had not been on leaving as much as on wondering what had caused such an attractive woman to cut out an entire side of her personality.

"I really haven't given it much thought," he admitted. "My mind's been on other things since I returned." The look he gave Ashley let her know where his mind had been.

"Do you think we can contact anyone tonight?"

"I have no doubt I can reach someone. The question is, can I give directions specific enough to enable someone to find this place? The roads up here don't seem to have many street signs." Ashley recalled the many roads they had passed and knew that without a map, a person unfamiliar with the area would only get lost.

Rafe leaned back in his chair. "I have a suggestion to make. Why don't we wait another night before doing anything? If we haven't heard from Tysinger by, say, noon tomorrow, I'll confront Mrs. Krueger about getting a message out." He glanced at her sitting there looking so aloof, making no comment. He shrugged. "At least then we'll be moving around in daylight hours, which would be much more sensible than feeling our way along at night. How do you feel about spending another night up here?"

Ashley had expected the suggestion. Waiting for daylight made a lot more sense. "I don't see that we have much choice."

"Then I'm glad to know we've managed to find some subject on which we agree."

She lifted her head from staring into her wine-glass. "Do you find me that difficult to get along with?" She sounded almost shocked.

His lazy grin caused her stomach to do a sudden flip. "I refuse to answer on the grounds that whatever I say will no doubt start another argument, and I'm feeling too peaceful at the moment." He lounged there looking for all the world as though his only concern was how to spend the evening. As a matter of fact, that was her concern as well. Something told Ashley they might have opposing views on the subject.

She glanced at her watch. "I realize it's rather early, but I think I'll go on to bed."

"Suit yourself." He sounded bored. "I think I'll build a fire and enjoy the atmosphere for a while." He rolled his head against the sofa so that she was in his line of vision. "You're welcome to join me if you'd like."

She sat there wavering. To be honest, and she was forcing herself to at least be *that,* she wasn't ready for bed. But then, she wasn't ready to continue a romantic evening in front of a fire with Rafe, either. "Well, maybe I'll stay a while longer."

She noted that he didn't stand up and cheer, but what had she expected? She'd made her message clear, and he no doubt felt that the matter was closed.

Ashley was annoyed that her nerves seemed to be on edge, her skin was flushed, and her pulse was racing. Perhaps another glass of wine would help to relax her.

Ashley was amazed to find how much the wine had
on the sofa, it was Willing to ... For Ashley it's
glass dangling from a her hand with an in ...

Chapter Five

Ashley was amazed to find how much the wine had
relaxed her. She lay on her stomach, stretched full
length on the sofa with her shoes off and an empty
wine glass dangling from one hand. She had been
listening to Rafe's anecdotes about his past.

"You mean you actually jumped a freighter at
sixteen to prove to your father that you were a
man?"

"Yep. I figured he was too old and stodgy to understand what life was all about, so after one of our
many verbal battles I slammed out of the house,
hitchhiked to San Francisco, lied about my age, and
headed for Japan on a freighter." Rafe was stretched
out on the hearth rug, propped up on an elbow, di-

viding his time between watching Ashley and watching the fire as it began to settle into a glow of hot ashes.

"Weren't you scared?"

"If I was, I wouldn't admit it to anyone, especially not to myself. Hell, I was convinced I knew all there was to know. I didn't need to finish school." He paused. "Come to think of it, I think that's what started that particular argument. My dad had found out I'd been skipping some of my more boring classes." He grinned at the memory.

"What did your mother do?"

"What could she do? She tried to get us both to calm down and be reasonable. Coming from my mother, that should have broken us both up right there. However, my sense of humor hadn't reached the point where I could laugh at myself."

"But now it has?" Ashley asked with a smile.

Rafe's eyes rested on her face as the dying firelight created multicolored patterns across its surface. "I think so, yes." He continued to study her, and the thought came to him that he'd rarely seen a lovelier woman. She seemed to be unaware of the beauty that radiated from her. He felt his body reacting to her presence and admitted to himself that he wanted to make love to her.

"You're staring."

"I know."

"Do I have soot on my face?" She laughed softly, her earlier feelings of unease forgotten in the camaraderie of the evening. Why hadn't she liked this man, she wondered in surprise? She found him delightful. He'd allowed her to see his vulnerability, perhaps because he was comfortable with who he was. Funny, she'd noticed that only this evening.

A big yawn overtook her. She looked at her watch and laughed. "It's after midnight, and I'd planned to go to bed at nine."

He watched her mouth as it turned up in a soft smile. "I'm glad you didn't."

Her smile widened. "Me too, but I really do need to get some sleep. You were right when you pointed out that I'm not a morning person. But I want to get up early in case we have a day of hiking ahead of us."

Rafe groaned at the thought and rolled over onto his back. His shirt crept up on his stomach so that dark hair showed as it swirled into a T-shape and disappeared into his jeans. The snug pants outlined his shape. Ashley's eyes jerked back to his waist, but that didn't help much. She had an almost irresistible impulse to place her lips along that bared portion of his anatomy and plant kisses across the brown expanse. She eyed her empty wine glass with disfavor.

"How long was it before you went back home?" she asked, attempting to distract her mind from its erotic wandering.

"I was gone for two years before I had the guts to face my dad and admit I'd been wrong. That was the hardest thing I've ever had to do in my life." He shook his head. "I'll never forget it."

"Was he surprised?"

"Shocked, actually. I've never been one who could admit to being wrong, you see. That was the day I took my first step toward maturity." He was silent for a moment, lost in his memories. "Somehow I always knew he was there with me every step of the way."

Ashley's eyes drifted shut, then popped open. She sat up and stretched. "I think I'll go on to bed." She waited for his comment, but he was silent. She looked down at him lying at her feet and poked a bare toe into his ribs. "What are you going to do?"

The look he gave her made a mockery of the question, but she was determined to be the one to break eye contact. She was a novice at the badinage they'd enjoyed all evening, but she'd discovered she liked it and refused to back down.

"Oh, I'll probably go to sleep shortly. I think that sofa is long enough to hold me—unless you have a better suggestion." His eyes dared her to comment.

She looked at him, then at the sofa. "I'm sure you'll be quite comfortable. I'll even find you some extra blankets so you don't get too cold tonight." As she turned to leave the room, she heard his soft

"Good night, Ms. Allison" and turned back. He hadn't changed position, but he was watching her with a grin. She made a formal curtsy.

"Good night, Mr. McCord," she replied, and disappeared down the hallway.

Moonlight glowed through the glass wall in the guest bedroom. Ashley didn't need a lamp as she removed her clothes and hung them in the closet. They would probably have to be worn again tomorrow. She drifted into the bathroom, smiling to herself as she remembered some of Rafe's tales. She felt too keyed up to sleep and had decided that a nice, hot bath was just what she needed to relax her.

She piled her hair on top of her head and haphazardly stuck pins she'd found in her purse into various curls. Oh, how she wished for some moisturizing cream. Her face felt like sandpaper. Next kidnapping, she'd insist on it.

While rummaging in the bathroom cabinet for a face cloth, Ashley found a large container of bath oil and ended up dumping most of it into the hot water filling the tub. At that rate she'd slide right into bed and promptly slide right off it again. *Ashley*—she stared at herself in the mirror—*you never do anything in moderation.* Her image solemnly stared back. *You wait until you're twenty-eight years old before developing your very first crush. You idiot.*

I wonder if I'd be as attracted to him if I'd just met him in the normal course of events? Who knows? But he's managed to break through more of my defenses than anyone before.

The warm water caressed Ashley's skin, the oil causing the water to feel like liquid silk. She was aware of her body, as though Rafe's hands touched her everywhere the water lapped.

Enough of that! Much more and not only will you not be getting any sleep tonight, you'll be begging him not to sleep on the couch—and that would never do. Thank God he was self-assured enough not to feel threatened just because she'd made it clear that she had no intention of playing house. She nodded firmly and several curls slipped down onto her face.

As she stepped out of the cooling water, she noticed her small stack of underwear. It had to be rinsed out, but that would leave her with nothing to sleep in. Shrugging her shoulders, she filled the sink, added some face soap to the water and washed and rinsed her underthings. As she draped her lingerie over one of the towel racks, she smiled at the thought of Rafe coming in to wash and dry his face and grabbing a handful of slip. He wanted to experience marriage, did he?

Ashley wrapped a towel around herself, turned off the light, and opened the bathroom door with caution. The room was still moonlit, although the moon had moved higher in the sky. She glanced over at the undisturbed bed. What had she expected?

Ashley searched through the dresser for a suitable garment to sleep in. She pulled out a soft T-shirt, glad to see that it fell modestly to her thighs. The rest of the pins tumbled out of her hair as she flicked her small hairbrush through it. She could hardly hold her eyes open as she pulled back the covers and crawled into bed. She was sound asleep before her head hit the pillow.

The room was in dark shadow when Rafe came silently into the bedroom. He moved over to the bed of blankets and checked Josh. There was still enough light to show him Ashley's face as she slept, and he moved to the side of the bed as though drawn by an invisible cord.

She slept on her side with one hand tucked under her cheek, her hair in disarray on the pillow. He could feel deep within him the painful desire that he'd fought all evening. He couldn't understand his reaction to her—she wasn't the type of woman he admired. She was too independent, too opinionated and, if he were honest with himself, too virginal for his taste.

His women had several things in common. They were beautiful, eager to please, and understood their place in his life. Ashley certainly met the first criterion, but after that, she totally missed the mark. *So why do I have this irresistible desire to take her in my arms and coax from her the passion I've seen hints of?*

He sat down on the side of the bed and with a light touch brushed her hair from her ear. *An irresistible desire* . . . Rafe leaned over and kissed her softly just below the ear. Ashley murmured something and turned her head, her mouth a hairbreadth from his. He settled his lips on hers with a delicate touch, no longer thinking about his actions.

Ashley's mouth moved against his. She lifted her arms languidly to his shoulders as he deepened the kiss. His tongue sought the entrance it wanted and Ashley accommodated, her mouth shaping itself to his, her arms tightening around his shoulders. Without loosening his hold, Rafe shifted on the bed until he lay beside her, his arm slipping under her as he began to stroke her body. Her response sent electrical impulses throughout his system. The pounding of his pulse shook his body. His hand explored her sweet curves, finally settling on her breast, chastely covered by the T-shirt. He knew he must stop—he'd never intended to take advantage of her, but her lips were sweet—so sweet. Just a moment more, then he would leave her.

The spicy scent of Rafe's aftershave lotion stole into Ashley's dream. She was back in the forest, following the long, tunneled trail, trying to find her way. She was lost and panic began to overwhelm her attempts to be rational. Where was Rafe? He was supposed to be up ahead. How would she get out from among the endless trees?

Then she saw him. She'd been frightened and felt abandoned, and he'd come to find her. Unhindered by shyness, she ran toward him, acknowledging her need for him. She threw herself into his arms and pressed her head against his chest, loving the closeness of his body, wanting to absorb him through her very pores. She never wanted to be alone again.

He lifted her face with gentle hands and fit his mouth to hers. His fingers danced lightly across her face, soft touches upon her closed eyelids, over her cheeks and down to her shoulders.

He needed her as well. He told her that by the way he held her, kissed her, and stroked her. Ashley wrapped her arms around him as she melted against him, opening her mouth to his invasion.

The cedar-touched air and his spicy scent intermingled. His hands moved with more urgent caresses, outlining the curve of her hips—pulling her closer to his male need. Ashley drifted with him into the soft, silent night of sensations and physical yearnings she'd never before experienced.

He turned her in a gentle movement; his feather touch exploring the shape of her breast.

Her breast!

Ashley realized that she was no longer dreaming. Rafe was in bed with her, his arms wrapped around her, his mouth moving with heart-stopping touches along her throat, down the V-neck of her shirt. And she wasn't stopping him! In fact, her hands were exploring the rugged strength of his shoulder, exulting in the feel of his body.

"No!" She shoved him away from her.

Rafe had forgotten how the kiss had started. He only remembered her response—the warm, passionate response that he had known was there. He'd found it. Her sudden withdrawal left him stunned.

"Get out of this bed!" she demanded in a whispered hiss.

Rafe sat up, trying to gain control of his runaway emotions.

"What's your excuse this time, Mr. McCord? Didn't I bring you enough blankets, or did you need your mommy's good-night kiss before you could sleep?" she demanded, her anger intensified by the knowledge of her own arousal. How *dare* he do this to her!

Her words stung and he stood up, pulling his shirt down to his waist. "My mother never gave me a kiss like that! That must have been some dream you were having, lady."

Remembering her dream, she was further incensed. "Get out of here, do you hear me?"

"Oh, I hear you, all right. It's a wonder Josh hasn't."

She clamped her hand over her mouth but her eyes continued to scream at him. She sat there until he left the room, then fell back on her pillow.

Her body still quivered from his touch. She ached with the needs he had aroused in her. Damn him! What kind of man would take advantage of a sleeping woman, regardless of what she was dreaming? It was a long time before Ashley fell asleep again.

What kind of man would take advantage of a sleeping woman? Rafe paced the living room floor, disgusted with his actions, tied in knots with unsatisfied needs. *My God, she might have had to add rape to her list of outrages for the weekend if she hadn't realized what was happening.* Rafe knew he wouldn't be able to forgive himself for his loss of control. But more important to him at the moment was whether *she* would forgive him. He wouldn't have admitted it, but that question was more important to him than their need to leave the mountain retreat.

Ashley's eyes fluttered open and she saw daybreak. Mount Hood was a black silhouette, but the sky behind it changed from gray to pink as she lay there watching. Her eyes wandered to the recliner near the window, then blinked in surprise. Rafe sat there in profile, giving Josh his bottle.

The light filtering in was harsh on his face, showing heavy lines and deep circles under his eyes. He looked as though he hadn't slept at all. *I hope his conscience kept him awake!*

She continued to watch him, the knot in her chest dissolving as she noticed the loving way he held Josh. His expression was tender as he studied the tiny face of the baby energetically working on his first meal of the day.

Ashley had never seen her father or brothers hold or feed a baby. They loved their children—she knew that—but they would no more offer to help look after them, or nurture them, than they would expect one of the women to help brand cattle. Yet Rafe did it so naturally, as though he enjoyed it.

He's going to be a very handy father to have around.

Now where had that thought come from? He probably *would* be a good father, of course, with all the practice he was getting, but it certainly had nothing to do with her. She drifted off to sleep and dreamed of little boys with black curls and light blue eyes calling to her.

The next time she awoke, she was alone. Subdued, she crawled out of bed and took her shower. She leaned into the water as it began to run warm, then hot, unconscious of the luxury of hot water that far from civilization. She stood there with eyes closed, sudsing her hair, wishing she could return home and forget the weekend.

Rafe was standing looking out of the window and holding a cup of coffee, when Ashley walked into the kitchen. He turned, his face an impersonal mask. "Coffee's ready. Mrs. Krueger has Josh. I thought that would give us a chance to discuss a few things."

Ashley's heart started pounding. What could they possibly have to discuss at this point? Hadn't they said it all the night before? She poured a cup of coffee and glanced out of the window. The view was unbelievable.

"I know it doesn't erase what happened, but I want to apologize for my behavior last night." His voice was low, as though he found the words painful.

She turned away from the window and realized that Rafe had moved closer. She felt drawn to him and wanted nothing more than to rest her head on his shoulder. She found the thought annoying and straightened to her full height, determined to face the situation in an objective manner.

"Apology accepted. Can we talk about something else?"

"Dammit, Ashley, I mean it. I don't want you to think I'm the kind of guy who waits until his victim is asleep and then has his sinister way with her pure and innocent body!''

His tone of disgust was too much. She started laughing. ''Believe me, Rafe, that isn't what I was thinking. As a matter of fact, that *was* some dream you interrupted.'' Her cheeks flushed at the memory.

She really wasn't angry. He couldn't believe it. Most women would have had his hide tacked to the barn door by now. Or at the very least had their fathers out looking for him.

''I'm sure it's obvious to you that I'm not very experienced in these matters,'' Ashley said. ''I've never reacted to a man as I have to you, and I don't understand it.'' She managed to raise her eyes and face him, only to lose her train of thought when she saw the warmth and tenderness in his.

A smile began in his incredibly silver blue eyes and spread to his lips, curling them in an endearing way. ''Does this mean I haven't totally turned you off men forever?''

''Not exactly. It means that I will be in better control of my reactions in the future. I don't intend to get carried away again—with you or anyone.''

''But Ashley, what happened last night wasn't wrong. Premature, perhaps, but our reactions to each other are natural and normal.''

She moved away from him. In crisp tones she answered, "I'm sorry, but I don't buy that rationale." She waved her hand as he started to speak. "I appreciate your trying to smooth things over, though. I'm sure you're not used to getting this kind of reaction the morning after. It must be hard on your ego."

His eyes hardened as he clamped down slowly on a retort. Taking a deep breath, he spoke in a slow, clear voice. "Let's leave my ego out of the discussion, if you don't mind. All I'm saying is that you don't have to go into a convent or do penance for the rest of your life." He stood up and moved to the door of the kitchen. "You managed to prove you're like the rest of us. Welcome to the human race!"

"I *know* that. I told you I'm not blaming you, so why are you getting so angry?"

"I don't know!" he shouted. "You manage to get under my skin quicker than anybody I've ever known!" They glared at each other across the room, tension stretched taut between them.

The sound of car doors slamming broke the tension and Rafe spun around, heading for the window overlooking the trail.

"It's Tysinger and his companions. He doesn't look very happy."

Rafe and Ashley were in the living room when Tysinger entered the house. He was very quiet. They heard the muffled click of the door as it closed, then silence.

He walked into the room and stood there looking at them. The dapper man they had met on Friday was gone. This man had aged twenty years. His eyes burned with a rage that caused a quiver to shoot down Ashley's spine.

He looked at Rafe. "Who are you?" Never had a soft tone been so menacing.

"Raphael McCord."

"Are you Raul's brother?"

"Yes."

"I see." Tysinger moved away from them toward the sliding glass doors. He stood there for a moment, staring, then turned back to them. "You will no doubt be pleased to learn that your brother and his wife—" his eyes cut to Ashley, then back to Rafe "—managed to meet with Senator Hensley this weekend. So your little game was successful."

His eyes touched Ashley once again, the rage barely under control. "I happen to know Ralph Begley very well, Ms. Allison." A feeling of foreboding began to stir within Ashley. "We go back a long way together, so when you told me you worked with him, I decided to give him a call. He passed on some very interesting information."

Ashley knew what was coming. Ralph Begley was one of the most conservative attorneys in the state—

in his practice, his politics, and his personal beliefs. He was the one who had kept the firm from hiring women attorneys for years. Ashley knew he was her biggest hurdle to becoming a partner in the firm. And he was a friend of Tysinger's!

"Begley tells me you are known for your cool head and sharp wit. He also informs me that as far as he knows you are not married and have never been married. He was quite interested to hear the details of your romantic weekend with Mr. McCord."

Chapter Six

The ride back to town was completed in silence. Tysinger had made no objection to their leaving immediately, for which Rafe was thankful. He had a feeling they hadn't heard the last of Tysinger. He kept an eye on Ashley as she gazed out of the window. She had lost all color when Tysinger mentioned discussing her with her boss. Surely in this day and age nobody cared about an employee's personal life, but why else would she have shown such a reaction? She had handled the weekend so well, never breaking down, ready with a snappy retort, but Tysinger's news seemed to throw her.

He had no one but himself to blame. *Yes, Mc-Cord, you've managed to create quite a lot of havoc in people's lives, including your own, in one short weekend.*

What did he intend to do about it? He couldn't leave her to face the situation alone. She'd already explained that her law practice was her life. Could her career really be in jeopardy? He was going to have to get some answers from her.

They were dropped off in front of their office building, and Rafe spoke for the first time since they'd left the mountain.

"Where's your car?"

"At home. I rode the bus on Friday."

"I'll take you home."

"That's all right—"

"Ashley, it really isn't necessary to argue about *everything*. I said I'd take you home." He grasped her forearm in a firm grip as they walked to his car.

Other than giving directions, Ashley said nothing more on the way. When they had pulled into the driveway of her remodeled Victorian house and stopped, she started to hand Josh to Rafe.

"I want to go in with you to make certain everything is all right."

"Why shouldn't everything be all right? I've only been gone a couple of days."

"Indulge me, will you? Besides, we didn't finish our earlier discussion."

She stepped out of the car, careful not to awaken the sleeping baby. Rafe slid Josh from her shoulder, then followed her up the steps.

"I can't think of a thing that needs to be discussed at this point. I'm just glad the weekend is behind us and can be forgotten." She unlocked the door and swung it open, then came to an abrupt halt just inside the doorway.

The living room was a shambles. A lamp was overturned on one of the end tables. The oil painting over the fireplace hung at an angle. Papers, magazines, and a couple of figurines that had been sitting on Ashley's rosewood desk littered the floor.

Rafe acted first. "Let's report this to the police right away. Can you tell what's missing?" He started searching for her phone.

Ashley stopped him. "Don't call the police. There isn't anything missing." How was she ever going to explain?

"Dammit, Ashley, how can you be so blasted calm? Your house has either been burglarized, vandalized, or both, and you don't even want to let the police know?" Rafe looked at her as though she'd suddenly sprouted another head.

"Tasha did this, Rafe. She doesn't like to be left alone."

"Well, in that case my friend, it's my strong suggestion that you find some sort of treatment or counseling for your roommate." He waved his hand at the room for emphasis. "This is obviously the result of a very sick mind." Rafe pushed his hand through his hair as he gazed around in disbelief. "Why do you put up with it, for God's sake? If she's this violent now, there's no telling when she might turn on you." Josh had long since been awakened by Rafe's tirade as he stalked about the room, inspecting the damage. The baby's sleepy expression of puzzlement was almost more than Ashley could handle.

"Rafe." She tried to keep a straight face. "Tasha is my Siamese cat. She's really very gentle and lovable, but she just doesn't like staying alone." His eyes narrowed as he listened to her explanation. "She's grown used to being here all day by herself, but if I'm not home in the evening she gets upset. When she gets upset she likes to tear through the house. I've never left her on her own for a weekend before." She glanced around the room. "She's probably waiting in my bedroom right now expecting me to coax her out of her mood."

Rafe stared at her in disbelief. "Tasha is a cat?"

"That's what I said, Rafe."

"Your Oriental roommate is a cat?" he repeated, his voice climbing slightly.

A slight quiver in her voice gave Ashley's amusement away. "Well, I didn't know why you wanted to know who I lived with, and I thought it safer if you thought there was someone who might worry.''

Rafe might have been able to accept her explanation at another time, but he'd just had one hell of a scare. In fact, he had discovered that he wanted the right to protect this woman, and she found the whole scene hilariously funny! ''Well, Ms. Allison, you must have gotten your fair share of laughs this weekend, all at my expense. I've spent the weekend worrying about how to protect you from the situation I'd gotten us into. Now that's the laugh of the week—''

For the first time since Ashley had met him, Josh let out a wail. The loud voices were too much for him. His angry face so resembled the flushed countenance of his uncle that Ashley could no longer contain herself. She collapsed into a chair laughing.

Even Rafe's anger couldn't hold out against her infectious laughter and, as he hastily patted the sobbing infant, his grin began to appear. Before long he was laughing with her, the subdued baby totally bewildered by the incomprehensible behavior of the adults around him.

''I'm so sorry for laughing, Rafe—I know it isn't funny,'' Ashley finally managed to say. She wiped the tears from her eyes as she sat up. ''Part of it is just being so glad that the only casualty of the weekend was my living room." She sobered as she stared at him. "It could have been much worse."

"Yes, I know. But I'm not convinced the house is the only casualty. That's what I think we need to discuss." He took the blanket from around Josh and spread it on the area rug in front of Ashley's fireplace, then placed the baby on his stomach on the blanket.

"What do you mean?"

"What is Ralph Begley's reaction going to be concerning Tysinger's attempt to embarrass you?" He watched her closely and noticed how quickly she schooled her face to a bland expression.

"It's hard to say at this point, but I'm sure I'll find out tomorrow. It's nothing to concern you, though."

"Wrong. It directly concerns me. I caused the problem in the first place."

"Okay. I'll explain that to Mr. Begley. I'm sure he'll understand." She smiled brightly and stood up. "I know you're as anxious as I was to get home. Don't let me keep you."

Frustrated, Rafe got to his feet. "Look, why don't we have dinner together tonight. I've got a glimmer of an idea how we can resolve the problem so that Begley is satisfied." He leaned over and picked up Josh. "I want to think it through a little more before I let a cross-examining attorney get hold of it."

He smiled, his eyes filled with a warmth that suddenly reminded Ashley of the night before.

"What will you do with Josh?"

"Jeanine's mom will keep him. She plans to take care of him when I leave for California." He waited. "What do you say?"

She didn't want to see him walk out of her life. In three days he had managed to turn her sane and sensible world into a whirling mass of emotions she never knew existed. She would be much better off never seeing him again. "Dinner sounds fine. What time?"

Rafe opened the front door, then paused. "I'll be here around seven—see you then." The door closed quietly behind him.

Ashley stood staring at the door for long minutes after he left. What was happening to her? She felt as though she'd visited another planet and had just been beamed back to earth. Wandering into her bedroom she was greeted by an outraged cat. Tasha met her, tail high in the air, indignation in every line of her feline body.

"I know, Tasha. I abandoned you and I'm sorry." Ashley peeled off her clothes and padded barefoot into the bathroom where she began to fill the tub. Tasha followed, detailing her list of complaints and emphasizing them with sweeping exclamations of her tail.

"Quit throwing me those obscene gestures, if you don't mind," Ashley added as she slipped into the heated water. As she lay there soaking, her mind wandered back to all that had happened since Friday night. Discovering that she was capable of the passion Rafe had aroused in her had come as a distinct shock. She wasn't at all sure she was capable of forgetting the experience and continuing her life as though she'd never met him.

She knew she had to try.

"Get married!" Ashley's startled exclamation caused several heads to turn in the dimly lit dining room of one of Portland's finest hotels. Her face flamed as she watched the amused expression on Rafe's face. He wasn't even embarrassed by everyone looking in their direction.

"You don't have to act as though I just made an indecent suggestion, Ashley. Marriage is a perfectly respectable institution."

"That's not funny, Rafe."

"I don't mean it to be funny, Ashley. I'm serious."

"But why?" Ashley wailed.

"Come on, counselor, surely the reasons are obvious."

Ashley fumbled for her wine glass, took a hasty sip, then returned the glass to the table with careful deliberation. "Perhaps you should explain them to me anyway."

Rafe had spent the afternoon planning how best to approach the subject. The idea had first come to him during a sleepless night and he had pushed it from him, convinced that his guilty conscience was over-reacting. But the more he thought about it, the better he liked the idea. They didn't have to enter into any "death-do-us-part" relationship, but it would give Ashley credibility with her boss, and her job was her first priority, it seemed. He ignored the fact that he would also be able to enjoy all her delectable attributes without apology once they were married.

"All right. I postponed my meeting in San Francisco tomorrow. I could meet you at the courthouse as soon as it opens in the morning. We could get our license and find a judge to marry us. Then if Begley tries to give you a hard time, you can tell him we're married. He doesn't need to know for how long."

He was serious. Ashley studied the intent expression on Rafe's face as he explained his plan. Serious, concise, and devastating. No one had warned her how lethal to her sensible life the charm of a dynamic man could be. She felt like a drowning person going down for the third time.

"But, Rafe, I don't want to be married. I've never had any desire to be married. I've seen what it does to a woman. She spends all her time providing for everyone else's needs, with no life of her own. I can't be that way." Her eyes met his in a steady gaze. "I could never make such a commitment to anyone. Call me selfish—or self-centered—or too ambitious. Call it whatever you want, but I can't be that way. I don't even want to try."

"Does it have to be a permanent arrangement with you?"

"You mean marriage?"

"Yes. We'd only have to stay married long enough to protect your position at your office." He watched the emotions reflected in her expression and waited. He knew the importance of timing, and he used the knowledge with consummate skill.

"Let's dance while you think about it," he said as he took her hand and led her to the dance floor. Ashley had never danced much, but within moments she found herself following Rafe's strong lead, and she began to relax against his lean, muscular body.

Rafe's gaze lingered on her face as her eyes refused to meet his. It took all his restraint not to drag her to a secluded corner and kiss her until she agreed to marry him. Although the idea of marriage was new, he was eager to experience it with Ashley. It never occurred to him to wonder why.

When they returned to their table in silence, Rafe suggested that they leave. He wanted privacy to discuss the matter. When they walked into Ashley's house, Rafe paused in the doorway of the living room, taking in the total picture. "I must admit I prefer your decorating to Tasha's. She may be exotic, but a trifle wild with some of her ideas."

Ashley smiled, but her mind was obviously on other things.

"Where is Tasha, by the way?"

"In the bedroom, probably."

"I really think she and I ought to get acquainted." He wandered into the room and slid out of the soft blue suede jacket he wore. Loosening his tie, he opened the first few buttons of his shirt. "Ahhh, that's much better. Hope you don't mind my getting comfortable."

Ashley waved a hand. "Be my guest."

"So what do you think of my suggestion?"

"I don't think it would work."

"Why?"

"Do we have time to go into all the reasons or shall I skim over the top?"

Rafe sat down in a large, overstuffed chair and grinned. "If it's going to take a while, would you mind if I had a drink as...uh...fortification, perhaps?"

"Certainly. What would you like?"

"Do you have any brandy? I have a feeling I'll also need something reviving."

She disappeared into the kitchen. A few minutes later she returned holding two brandy snifters with generous measures of brandy in each.

He glanced at the amounts in each glass. "I said reviving, Ashley, not embalming." He shrugged his shoulders and settled back into his comfortable pose, sipping his drink.

Ashley took a rather large gulp of brandy and choked. Maybe she should have chose something a little milder, but it was too late now. She began to pace.

"All the reasons I gave at the restaurant are valid. I am not a homemaker. I have no desire to become a homemaker." She spun around. "I can't even cook, and believe me, in this day and age, it takes a tremendous amount of skill to avoid learning how to cook."

He started laughing.

"It isn't funny. Besides that, we don't know each other. This is only the second time we've been together."

"That's true, but our first meeting was a blockbuster." He stood up, gently pulling her into his arms. "I'm not going to ask you for anything you don't want to give me, Ashley. I thought you knew me well enough by now to understand that. If you really hate the relationship, we can call it off with no hard feelings. Surely you don't find an offer like that threatening, do you?''

She was so confused. Everything he said made sense. Without the protection of a marriage, she might very well lose her chance to move up in the firm. She was making it sound as though marriage would be a real sacrifice for her. Then she remembered how this man could affect her and she stiffened. If she were ever to experience his lovemaking, she knew she'd never be able to end the relationship.

Finally, she nodded. Before she could say a word Rafe tightened his arms around her, giving her a kiss that claimed his possession of her. ''Then you'll marry me?'' he murmured, his hands smoothing the silky material covering her back.

She pulled back from him, determined to be honest with him. ''I know what you're doing, Rafe, and I really appreciate it. You're determined to play the role of my knight come to rescue me.''

His face flushed. He wasn't that saintly.

''Because it's so very important for me not to jeopardize my job, I'll marry you on a temporary basis.'' He started to pull her to him once more but she resisted. ''But it will have to be a marriage in name only.''

Chapter Seven

Ashley glanced at her watch as she left her office. It was a few minutes after five. She smiled. Leaving on time had become a habit since Rafe McCord had entered her life. Nothing had been the same since the weekend she'd spent on the mountain six weeks earlier.

They had followed Rafe's plan and gotten married the Monday after they met. Rafe's instincts had been sound. Ashley had no sooner arrived in her office that Monday than the phone rang.

"Ashley," a male voice intoned, "this is Ralph Begley. If you have a few minutes, I'd like to see you."

"Certainly, sir. I'll be right there." She flicked a comb through her hair, straightened the bow on her blouse, and walked to Ralph Begley's corner office.

Tapping on the door, she entered dutifully at his command. Two walls of glass provided views of Mount Hood and Mount Saint Helens and, in the foreground, the Willamette River curving around the downtown area like a snake.

"Ashley, come in. I appreciate your taking the time to see me." He motioned to one of the chairs. She took a seat and waited.

Ralph Begley looked larger than life. White wavy hair framed his aristocratic face. A heavy jawline gave him something of the look of a bulldog, and from his reputation Ashley understood him to be as tenacious as one.

"You may not be aware that Virgil Tysinger and I are close personal friends."

Here it comes. She attempted a smile. "So he mentioned this weekend, sir."

He looked startled at her easy admission. "Then you admit to being at his mountain retreat this weekend."

Ashley feigned a puzzled expression. "Why yes, sir. My husband and I had the pleasure of being Mr. Tysinger's guests. He has a beautiful place, but then I'm sure you know that."

The conversation was obviously not progressing along the lines Begley had planned. "Uh, no, as a matter of fact, I've never been there. Uh, Ashley, I wasn't aware you were married."

She smiled. "Oh, yes, but we haven't mentioned it to many people, and I intend to continue using my maiden name professionally."

"Is there a particular reason you don't want it known, Ashley?"

Hang on to the ole temper, girl. He's trying to bait you, and you're too smart for that. "No. As a matter of fact, as soon as Rafe finishes his business in California we intend to have a reception for all our friends and family." Smile firmly in place, she added, "You'll receive one of the first invitations." If only he were aware of his role as Cupid in their hasty merger!

Begley reminded Ashley of a clipper ship sailing before a wind that has suddenly failed, leaving it becalmed on a motionless sea. She returned to her office mentally praising Rafe for his foresight.

When Rafe called that evening he seemed pleased that his tactics had been effective, and they discussed their next step. To be convincing, Rafe would need to spend some time with Ashley, and she agreed it was only sensible that he move in with her—on a temporary basis, of course. He had accepted her decision not to consummate the marriage, but Ashley was nervous at the thought of sharing her home with him.

She needn't have worried. Rafe arrived and good-naturedly moved into her guest room, then set about showing Ashley that her ideas of marriage needed revising. For one thing, Rafe was used to living alone and taking care of himself. Wonder of wonders, he didn't suddenly develop a helplessness that Ashley had always suspected occurred in the male promptly upon repeating his marriage vows.

He shared chores in the kitchen and other domestic duties with no hint of complaint and, once again, she tried unsuccessfully to picture her father or brothers doing a load of laundry or drying dishes.

Most important to Ashley, she was given the privacy she needed. She had trouble at first adjusting to his affectionate nature—his need to touch, his habit of hugging her to him, of stroking her shoulder whenever he walked by—but within a few short weeks she discovered how much she looked forward to his demonstrative behavior and tentatively began to respond.

So why was she beginning to feel on edge whenever Rafe was around and restless when he was gone? During the six weeks they'd been together, he'd flown to California once, for four days, and she and Tasha had wandered around the house as though lost.

Tasha had adopted Rafe within days of his arrival, much to Ashley's chagrin. She had explained to Rafe that Tasha did not take to strangers, that she carried aloofness to an extreme, and cautioned him not to be hurt when she ignored him. Hah! Tasha followed him everywhere he went, and Ashley suspected that she slept with him since she no longer turned up in Ashley's room at night.

Yes, Rafe had turned Ashley's sane and sensible world upside down, and she hesitated to think what adjustments she would have to make once the need for their marriage was past.

An unexpected bonus of her marriage was the acquisition of Raul and Jeanine as family. Once Ashley met Raul she could better understand the confusion that first weekend—the two men looked very much alike. However, in Ashley's opinion, Rafe had a compelling sensuality that was missing in Raul. Ashley felt comfortable and relaxed around Raul, restless and disturbed around Rafe. Jeanine reminded Ashley of Tinkerbell with short, black curls. She would never forget Jeanine's explanation of how she and Raul had met. . . .

"We met at Stanford University," Jeanine explained in her ebullient fashion. "I'm the world's greatest crusader for hopeless, helpless causes. Raul managed to extricate me from one that was about to be hit with a big scandal." She grinned, not at all repentent. "It did, too. My family was so grateful to him for running interference for me that they welcomed him into the fold." Her large, black eyes rolled. "For my family, that's really something." In a confiding tone, she whispered, "They were convinced that the only reason anyone would want to marry me was for my money."

The women had met for lunch, and Ashley almost choked on her iced tea. "Your money?"

"Yes. I come from a long line of moneyed Oregonians who believe in intermarriage with other moneyed Oregonians. It almost becomes incestuous after a while." Her eyes danced as she watched the expression on Ashley's face. "They recognized that Raul was different. We've laughed about it several times since then. The McCords could buy and sell our family out of their miscellaneous fund."

Nor would she forget Jeanine's explanation of how she had become involved in the southern Oregon investigation. : . .

"In my normal crusading spirit I got involved in the fight against the use of herbicides and volunteered to help gather data. You can imagine how surprised I was to discover that some of those anxious to fight the use of herbicides were growing marijuana. However, they weren't letting themselves be known and we needed specific information about them." She paused and took a drink of her coffee. "So I got this idea about going 'underground.'"

Ashley groaned.

"That was exactly Raul's reaction! But by the time he found out what I'd done, it was too late to back out." She shrugged her shoulders. "As long as I was involved, I stayed to find out what I could."

"But weren't you pregnant during that time?"

"Of course. That's what made my idea work. You see, I pretended my boyfriend had dumped me when I told him I was pregnant. The guy I named had been a dealer and was in jail awaiting trial on drug charges. I figured they wouldn't check up on my story—" she paused, her twinkling eyes sharing her amusement "—and I was right. I managed to find out quite a lot...."

Ashley had never known anyone quite like Jeanine, but she enjoyed her enormously, and they became friends.

Rafe rapidly became the focal point of Ashley's daily routine. He never crowded her, but he was there when she needed him. When things were hectic for her, she enjoyed sharing her day with him while she unwound. One of his most endearing traits was his ability to plan sudden trips to the coast or the mountains whenever she had free time. They spent a great deal of time laughing together; their sense of the ridiculous was a bond they shared.

However, the nights were becoming more difficult for Ashley. Knowing he was in the next room kept her tossing restlessly each night. He never suggested that he was dissatisfied with their arrangement, and she was embarrassed by her increased arousal whenever he was near. If Rafe was similarly afflicted, he hid it well.

She entered the front door and heard his voice and her stomach began to quiver in anticipation. "Rafe?"

"In here, love," he called from the kitchen. His casual use of endearments had been something else she had grown accustomed to. "Tasha's just been filling me in on your outrageous behavior."

Ashley stopped in the doorway of the kitchen and surveyed the scene. Rafe stood with one foot negligently crossed over the other as he leaned against the cabinet, arms folded over his chest. Tasha sat on one of the chairs facing him.

"What outrageous behavior?" Ashley demanded to know.

"She won't say," he admitted, his tone grave. "She just looks at me with a knowing expression and blinks when I ask for specifics."

"Don't fall for that—she practices her inscrutable expression before the mirror. Doesn't mean a thing."

He moved over to her, slipping his arms around her waist. As his lips moved toward hers, he whispered, "I've missed you today." His mouth found hers with unerring precision. As he fitted her snugly against his taut body, Ashley relaxed, enjoying the haven of his arms. Her mouth opened in unconscious invitation and his tongue took advantage, moving across her teeth and touching her with an intimacy that hinted of further delights, if she only dared to accept them. She could feel the acceleration of his heart under her palm. At least she was consoled to know she affected him too.

With reluctance he drew away. "We're invited to Raul and Jeanine's for dinner. I told them I'd let them know if you wanted to go out tonight—that it would depend on the kind of day you've had."

It wasn't fair. It wasn't good enough that he was handsome and sexy, he had to be sensitive and understanding too. Ashley knew that she had never stood a chance of resisting this man. If he only knew, she'd given up the struggle weeks ago.

"I'd enjoy dinner with them," Ashley murmured. "We haven't seen them in a while."

Rafe chuckled. "That's because I explained that since we're on our honeymoon, we prefer to keep to ourselves."

Ashley could feel the warmth move into her cheeks. "I'm sure this hasn't been quite your idea of a honeymoon." He continued to hold her closely against him, and she knew he was not unaffected by her nearness.

"Oh, I don't know," he said, mischief dancing in his incredibly blue eyes. "It certainly has had its moments."

Slowly disengaging herself from his arms, she tried for a casual tone. "Let me shower and change and I'll be ready to go."

Rafe watched her walk away, then went and poured himself a drink. *Much more of this frustration and I'm either going to turn into an alcoholic or a human prune from all the cold showers I've taken during the past six weeks.*

He had understood her reservations about their union. In fact, he agreed with them. They needed to get to know each other; that was why he had cancelled the delicate negotiations he'd been involved with in California. Since meeting Ashley, Rafe's priorities had undergone a subtle shift.

The most important task he had now was to win her trust. He was reminded of the summer he and Raul had managed to tame a young doe their grandfather had caught and penned. As long as they allowed her to make the approaches, they made progress. Eventually she would come and eat from their hands but continued to shy away whenever they attempted to touch her. Ashley was the same way. She was skittish whenever he attempted more than a casual embrace, and he patiently waited for her to come to him. The toll on his restraint had been tremendous.

Is it even worth it? he muttered to himself as he took a large swallow of bourbon and water. *All it would take is a phone call, and there would be someone waiting by the time my flight arrived in California tomorrow.* The imminent trip ate at him. The call had come that afternoon, and he knew he couldn't ignore it. How long did he intend to stay up here like a lovesick schoolboy waiting to be noticed? He had his own life to live, and from all indications Ashley was content to live hers without him.

His gamble of moving in with her had not paid off and he might as well accept it. He wondered whether she would even care that he had to return to his business interests. Finishing his drink, he set his glass down with deliberation. He didn't want another woman; he wanted Ashley. Somehow he'd pictured himself falling for a docile, homemaker type who would be content to raise his children and spend his money. Who would ever have believed that he'd fall for an independent, sassy-tongued witch who had the ability to turn him inside out with a flash of her smile or the sound of her laughter.

The ride to Raul and Jeanine's was quiet; each was lost in his or her own thoughts.

* * *

Ashley was listening to Jeanine describe Josh's latest feat when she heard a sentence of Rafe's conversation with Raul that caused her to hold her breath.

"I'm going to have to go back down there and see what I can save of the fiasco. It may already be too late, but I have to try." Rafe's voice was low, but Ashley caught every word.

So did Jeanine. "I didn't know you were going to have to return to California, Rafe. I thought your move up here was permanent."

Rafe's eyes found Ashley's trained on him, a question in their depths. He smiled at his sister-in-law. "Sounds great in theory, Jeanine, but unfortunately, all my investments are in California."

Raul caught the strain in Ashley's face. "Will you be able to go with him, Ashley?"

Three pairs of eyes speared her with their intentness. Why hadn't he mentioned that he was leaving? How long had he known? She shook her head. "No, I'm afraid there's no way I can leave right now. My court docket is filled for the next several weeks." She attempted a smile. "Of course, Rafe knows where to find me when he finishes his business in California."

"Well, the honeymoon had to end some time, I suppose," Raul offered with a grin. Unfortunately, his brother didn't find the remark amusing.

Jeanine was quick to change the subject and during the rest of the evening the conversation was light, for which Ashley was thankful. She had known that her relationship with Rafe had to end, but somehow she hadn't expected it to be over so soon. However, she had no intention of letting the others know how the news had affected her.

The tension between them was almost visible when Rafe and Ashley returned home. There was nothing to say, but Ashley made the attempt.

"When do you have to leave?"

Rafe was silent for so long that she thought he was going to ignore her question. At last he cleared his throat. "There's an eight-thirty flight in the morning that would put me into San Francisco in time for a meeting scheduled at ten."

They entered the house and Ashley absently went about the routine of feeding Tasha. Since Rafe's advent into their lives, Tasha had seemed to accept their occasional evenings away. Somehow Rafe had managed to hypnotize the cat into more civilized behavior.

When she returned to the living room, Ashley found Rafe staring out of the front window. A light from the hall was the only illumination.

Determined to get a grip on her emotions, Ashley decided to confront their situation. "I suppose our marriage has been accepted by now, so there's really no reason to prolong it, is there?"

She saw Rafe stiffen as she began to speak. He turned slowly, the light slanting across his face, leaving his eyes in shadow.

"What marriage?" he asked, his tone harsh.

"Rafe?" She was bewildered. "What's wrong?"

"I just find it amazing that you can discuss so unemotionally the end of something that never had a proper beginning."

"But Rafe, the whole idea was to protect my job, and our marriage accomplished that. I thought you'd be eager to resume your life in California by now."

In rapid strides Rafe moved to where she stood and clamped his arms on her shoulders. "You really do see me as some self-sacrificing knight who came to your rescue, don't you?"

Confused by the anger she could hear in his voice, she attempted to step back, and his hold tightened. "What other reason was there?"

"This!" He took her in his arms, his mouth taking hers in fierce possession. Ashley's arms locked behind his head and she returned his kiss passionately, running her hands through the curls at the nape of his neck, and loving the feel of her breasts pressed against him.

They were both breathless when Rafe broke their contact. In a tortured voice, Rafe spoke. "I made a promise to myself that night I almost took you that I would never make love to you unless you invited me to. That was the only way I knew to show you that you could trust me." He groaned as he nuzzled her neck. "But it's been hell living with you every day, seeing you, wanting you, and not being able to have you." He stopped and kissed her again as though starved for the taste of her. "I can't take any more of it, Ashley. I've got to get away from you before I break that promise and end up causing both of us to hate me."

Ashley's arms slid around Rafe's waist and she reveled in the feel of him. "Rafe, all you needed to do was tell me how you felt. I've lain there night after night fantasizing about what would happen if I were to get up and go to your room and beg you to love me." She placed quick kisses along his jaw line and his hands explored her spine, caressing the curves of her hips as though he planned to sculpt them. "I couldn't do it. As much as I wanted you, I couldn't ignore the ingrained inhibitions. I couldn't be so brazen as to force myself on you."

"*Force* yourself." He groaned. "Oh, Ashley, we've both been so ridiculous and wasted an unbelievable amount of time." Rafe scooped her into his arms, carrying her easily, and moved down the hallway to her room.

As he placed her on the bed, Ashley was certain that she smelled the soft scent of cedar intermingled with Rafe's aftershave lotion. She watched him as he removed his clothes down to his briefs, those incredibly tiny briefs that could not conceal the effect she had on him. Then he joined her on the bed.

She tensed as he touched her, unsure of the next step. "It's all right, love, I'm not going to rush you," he murmured as he slipped her blouse and skirt from her. He paused when scraps of lace were all that covered her and began to kiss her with long, drugging kisses. Her trembling ceased and she began to respond to his caresses. A slow fire started deep within her and she began to imitate his movements.

"Oh, yes, Ashley, touch me, love—I want to feel your hands on me."

His encouragement led her to further exploration and by the time he shifted his weight over her, she ached for his possession. She had never thought herself capable of experiencing the emotions Rafe stirred within her. His possession appeased a need that had been growing in her since their first weekend together. She gloried in the tremor she felt course through him, reassured that the overwhelming response she felt was shared. Ashley felt that nothing could equal the emotional high his lovemaking created until she heard Rafe murmur, "Dear God, how I love you, Ashley Allison McCord," and her heart overflowed.

After twenty-eight years, Ashley had found her home in Rafe's arms.

Chapter Eight

Autumn had left its calling card wherever Ashley looked; the yellow leaves of the sycamores and the red of the sumac dressed up lawns and parks. Brisk mornings warned that winter was beginning to stir from its summer hibernation.

Ashley had gotten into the habit of walking to work. She needed the exercise, and it gave her time to make the transition from her personal to her professional life. Not that there was much happening in her personal life at the moment. Rafe had been back to Oregon only twice since the night they had made their marriage a reality more than two months earlier. She lived on the memories of those visits, waiting for his return.

Rafe had called several times to see whether she could fly down to him, but she had always had to refuse. She was too close to making partner now to risk taking time to travel south. More than one partner had met with her during the past few weeks to discuss her feelings toward her practice and the firm, and to ask her about her goals. She was excited about her career, and only the knowledge that Rafe would arrive the next day gave her more pleasure than her job.

One more day. They'd been apart for more than three weeks. Something was going to have to give in their schedules soon.

About midmorning her phone rang. It was Raul. He had never called her at the office before, and her first thought was something had happened to Rafe.

Ashley's heart leaped, then started pounding. "Raul? Is something wrong?"

"Well, let's put it this way. I'm calling you in your professional capacity. I think I've been framed."

"Why? What's happened?"

"There was a chemical spill at the plant last week under rather peculiar circumstances. Today I've been served with papers from the Department of Environmental Quality asking that the court shut McCord Industries down." His voice sounded grim. "Since you happen to be my favorite lawyer, I wondered if I could make an appointment to see you and discuss the matter." He paused. "Will it hurt your feelings to know that you're also the *only* lawyer I know?"

Ashley laughed, relieved to know that Rafe was all right. "No, Raul, that doesn't hurt my feelings." She glanced at her calendar. "As a matter of fact, I've got a cancellation at eleven this morning. Why don't you bring the papers around and let me look at them?"

"That'll be great. I'll see you at eleven. Oh, and Ashley?"

"Yes?"

"Thanks." The receiver clicked.

Raul watched Ashley's face as she read the summons, complaint, and motion for temporary injunction. If granted, McCord Industries would have to shut down immediately, perhaps on a permanent basis.

"What can you tell me about the spill?" Ashley said, glancing up from the documents.

"Well, we have a number of drains that allow chemical waste to run off into holding tanks. The spill occurred because one of those drains was plugged."

"You think it was deliberate?"

"I know it was. I found a large piece of wood stuck in the drain. There's no way that piece of wood could have gotten in there accidentally."

"Have you talked with the employees who were at the plant when the spill happened?"

"More than once, and no one seems to know anything or to have seen anything. I'm completely baffled."

"It looks as if Tysinger's still at work, Raul."

"How could he be behind this, Ashley? He and several others have been indicted and are awaiting trial. What could he hope to gain?"

"Nothing. It's what he hopes you lose. He's obviously vindictive and could easily have bribed someone in your plant to cause trouble. I think you're right. You've been framed."

"So what do I do about it?"

"We fight it, that's what."

Raul took in the picture Ashley made. She looked as though she'd been energized, ready to go into orbit, to move mountains and leap rivers. She suddenly broke the silence. "The hardest part of all of this is the hearing for the injunction. That's only a week away, and we'll need as much time as possible to investigate your employees."

"What does the temporary injunction mean?"

"It means they think your business is a menace and so dangerous that the court should shut it down immediately until such time as a trial can be held so that a judge can hear the arguments and decide whether—" she ticked off on one finger "—you re-open the business, or—'' she touched another finger ''—you stay closed permanently.''

''If we should get closed down, how long before a trial?''

''A good question. It could be months. I don't think any business could stand that.''

Raul's face blanched. ''No. I'd miss too many contract deadlines. That would ruin me.''

''And that, dear brother,'' she said with a wink, ''is why I don't intend to let them win on their motion next week. So we've got a busy time ahead of us.'' She smiled, her air of confidence creating a feeling of confidence in him that she could do what she set out to do. For the first time since he'd been served with the papers that morning, Raul managed to take a deep breath and relax.

Ashley was relieved to see the tension ease in his face. She walked him to the door. ''See what kind of information you can get for us, then quit worrying about it. Remember, you've turned it over to your lawyer now, so let me do the worrying. That's what you pay me for.''

Raul stepped out of the office, then turned back to say, ''Now I can see the advantages of having a lawyer in the family, Ashley. You're going to be one of our greatest assets.'' Ashley could feel her face flush. What a thing to say in front of her secretary. He was almost as bad as Rafe. ''And you turn such pretty colors too. A really unusual addition, that's for sure.'' He walked down the hall laughing as Ashley smiled sheepishly at her secretary and dived for her office.

By the time Ashley got home that evening she was too excited to sleep. Rafe would be flying in sometime the next day. She decided to start reading the Robert Ludlum book she'd purchased some time ago. She would probably be sleepy after a couple of chapters. Wrong! Midnight found her in bed, propped up with pillows, avidly turning pages. Tasha perched herself on the pillow next to Ashley. The predicted rain had started in the afternoon, which had made her walk home a little damp but sounded very soothing as it tapped a merry rhythm on her bedroom windows.

The book had her total concentration, so she didn't hear the car drive up the rain-slicked street until it pulled into her drive and stopped. She lowered the book and checked the clock. It was after midnight.

The doorbell rang as she tugged on her warm housecoat and fished for her slippers. It rang again as she trotted down the hall. ''Who is it?''

''Rafe.''

She fumbled with the chain, yanking it away as she turned the handle of the door. She threw open the door and flew into his arms. "What are you doing here?"

The impact of her body knocked him back a pace or two, his arms instinctively holding her to him. "I thought I'd find you asleep this late at night. Is something wrong?"

She grabbed his hand and pulled him into the darkened house, the glow of the lamp from her bedroom providing enough light for them to see.

"I'm all right," she said with a hint of impatience, "but how come you're here early?" She led him into the bedroom, turned, and for the first time saw him in full light. Lines of weariness were etched across his face. "Rafe! What's happened?"

"Nothing's happened." He shrugged out of his jacket and pulled her back into his arms. "I just couldn't stand not seeing you for another day. I was in another interminable meeting today, listening as they cussed and discussed, and I realized that I no longer cared what happened." He pulled her closer, his hands wandering up and down her back, hungry for the feel of her. "So I got up, told them politely that I had to leave but would be in touch, then walked out to the car and started driving."

"You *drove* up here?" She couldn't believe it. "That's a good twelve-hour drive."

He gave her an endearing grin. "Well, I made it in better time than that, but you're right, it's a long drive." He started kissing her cheek and ear. "And I haven't been able to sleep for wanting you." His kiss left her in no doubt that she'd been needed. She felt so complete when he was holding her. The last few weeks had been tough for her and obviously for Rafe too. She'd never seen him look so drawn. He'd lost weight and there were deep circles under his eyes. "Oh, Rafe, what have you been doing to yourself?"

"Just trying to get back up here to you," he murmured, his hands finding the tie of her housecoat and pulling it open. He couldn't seem to touch her enough.

She pulled away from him. "Are you hungry? Can I fix you something to eat?"

His eyes seemed to be almost glazed. "I'm more thirsty than anything."

"Let me get you something, then. Are you sure you don't want a sandwich?" She unbuttoned his shirt and pulled it off his shoulders, then pushed him onto the bed.

"I don't care. A sandwich is fine." He lay back across the bed with a luxurious sigh. "I never knew a bed could feel so good." He lay there with his eyes closed.

Ashley rushed into the kitchen, prepared a sandwich in record time, poured a large glass of milk, put them on a tray, and dashed into the bedroom with the tray. Rafe was sprawled across the bed, asleep.

He'd taken his socks and shoes off, but his pants were only unsnapped at the waist. Tasha sat next to his shoulder, studying him with feline interest.

"So what do you think? Shall we keep him?" she asked Tasha. She set the tray down and worked his pants down his hips and legs. Rafe was a dead weight as she pushed and pulled him over to one side of the bed, then managed to pull the covers up over him.

She looked at the glass of milk, the sandwich, and the book on the bedside table. Then she looked at Rafe. He'd been trying to kill himself, she thought. Nothing was worth that.

She crawled back into bed with a smile, picked up the book, and continued to read, this time eating Rafe's sandwich and sipping his glass of milk.

Ashley finished the book a little after two. During that time, Rafe had not moved. She'd never seen a person sleep so soundly. *He must be exhausted.* For that matter, so was she. She should have known better! Turning off the light, she curled up to Rafe's back. He was home at last.

Sometime during the night Rafe turned over and pulled Ashley into the curl of his body. He woke up and found her in his arms. She looked like a young girl, her hair spread across the pillows, a contented smile on her face. Should he wake her? He knew she needed her rest, but the temptation was more than he could resist.

With a very light touch, Rafe ran his hand down her side from her ribs to the hollow of her waist, then over the curve of her hip. His hand slowed as it reached her thigh and began to drift inward. She leaned back into his warm body, then turned her head. Slowly lifting heavy eyelids, she murmured, "Good morning."

"It certainly is," he whispered and turned her more completely toward him. Her silken skin caused his hand to tremble as he caressed the hills and valleys of her body, warm from the covers. Her hands began their own exploration, reacquainting themselves with his body, which she was beginning to know as well as her own.

Rafe pulled the covers from her, wanting to enjoy the sight of her lying there waiting for him. He started placing kisses on her shoulder, then slid his mouth down to the breast waiting for his possession. His mouth covered the tip and he began to tease the nipple until Ashley could feel the reaction in her innermost body.

She reached for him but he resisted the pull of her arms as he began to taste her body. She remembered several ways to get his attention. Her hand softly stroked him, causing his flesh to quiver.

"Ashley," he groaned. As she continued to glide her hands over him, Rafe pulled her to him roughly. Their need proved greater than their patience, their merging more volcanic than gentle, more intense than pleasurable, their striving for unity more necessary than the ultimate fulfillment, but in that striving and seeking they were fortunate, and found it all.

The persistent ringing of the phone cut through the mists of sleep and Ashley felt for the phone by the bed.

"Hello?" Her voice sounded groggy.

"Good afternoon!" Jeanine bubbled. "Something tells me that Rafe has arrived. Sorry if I woke you from your nap." She didn't sound in the least sorry. She sounded more as though she were trying not to laugh.

Rafe stirred, then opened one eye.

"I'm calling to see if you and Rafe would like to come over for dinner."

"I'm not sure what this fireball of energy has planned, if anything. Shall I ask him?"

Jeanine chuckled. "By all means."

Turning to Rafe, Ashley explained. "Jeanine wants to know if we'd like to come over for dinner. She probably thinks I haven't planned much." She'd be right, for that matter. Eating was not on her list of priorities when Rafe was home. She reached over and brushed the hair away from his forehead.

He groaned and closed his eye. Ashley ran a hand through her hair and looked at the clock. It was after one o'clock. "I'm not sure I can interpret his groans right now, Jeanine. Why don't I call you back in a little while?" Rafe's head nodded into the pillow.

"No problem. We're going to be here and if you show up, I'll just throw on two more steaks."

Ashley placed the phone back on its stand. Rafe's hand began to move along her ribcage and over her stomach.

"I thought you were asleep." They were still in the same position they'd been in when they fell asleep, legs intertwined, Rafe's arm under her neck.

"I am." His eyes remained closed.

"At least I'll bet your arm is asleep. I must have cut off the circulation." She sat up and gingerly moved his arm.

"Ow! You're right. My fingers are numb." He moved them tentatively; one eye opened to watch.

Ashley managed to prop herself up on a pillow. She couldn't remember when she'd last slept so well. Rafe was much better than a sleeping pill.

She glanced down at the man lying beside her. "So what do you want to do?"

Both eyes opened and watched her for a moment. "I'm not sure. What sort of entertainment can you provide if we stay here?" His mouth turned up at the corners. She got off the bed, then glanced back at the sprawled male in her bed.

"Darned if I know. My entertainment director took the weekend off." She wandered into the bathroom and turned on the shower.

By the time she'd pinned up her hair, Rafe was already in the shower yelping as he tried to adjust the water flow. "My God, woman, doesn't this place run to hot water?"

Peeking into the shower, she laughed and said, "I knew I forgot to pay something. Must have been one of the utilities." The water was pleasantly warm when Ashley stepped in and grabbed the soap. Filling the washcloth with suds, she began to scrub the wide back before her. She heard a purr of pleasure. Then she stroked down over the startling white skin on his slim hips. "When I first met you I wondered if you were naturally bronzed all over." He turned around and tugged the washcloth from her hand.

"Disappointed?" His voice roughened as he began to cover her breasts and shoulders with soap.

"Nope. I'm rather impressed, actually." Her eyes were twinkling as she looked at him demurely from beneath her lashes.

He handed her back the soap and washcloth. "Since you started this, you might as well do my front, too." A definite gleam appeared in his eyes.

From this angle Ashley noted that his body had been stimulated by the shower—or something.

"Maybe I'd better let you do your own washing," she muttered as she vigorously soaped his chest and shoulders. "Here, you do the rest." She handed the cloth back to him and grabbed for the soap.

"Oh, no, that's not fair. You got to wash me, now it's my turn." He began to ease the washcloth over her body in long, nerve-tingling strokes, starting at her shoulders and slowly sliding down to her thighs. Ashley's response was all Rafe could have wanted. She gazed up at him, her eyelids heavy with desire, then she reached up to kiss him as his arms came around her.

"Oh, Rafe—"

It was several hours before she returned Jeanine's call to tell her that they would be over.

The rain that had started on Friday continued through the weekend. It was the steady, soaking rain that was so much a part of the fall and winter months in the Pacific Northwest. The rain tapping on the windowpanes provided a counterpoint to the spirited conversation around the dining table at Raul and Jeanine's. The impending lawsuit was the topic.

Raul told Rafe and Ashley the results of the investigation of his employees.

"I'm very much afraid James Jackson is involved in the accident," Raul said.

Rafe looked up from his plate. "But James has been your plant manager for the past five years. What would make you suspect him, of all people?"

"Nothing concrete, I'm afraid. Just a general attitude of surliness where there hadn't been one before—a defensiveness that seems out of character."

"Do you think he's the one who set up the accident, or that he knows who did?"

"I haven't a clue. Either way, it would end his career with us." He glanced at Ashley. "My counselor keeps telling me not to worry—that's what I pay her to do." He grinned, his resemblance to Rafe intensifying.

Rafe's eyes rested on Ashley with a warmth that caused her to shift in her chair. "So what do you think, counselor? Can we win this one?"

"We're going to do our best. The company's clean record over the past several years is a point in our favor. What we really need to do is to prove that the spill was, in fact, engineered. Why would one of your employees sabotage you like that?"

"That's what I can't figure out." Raul refilled their wine glasses as Jeanine took their plates into the kitchen. "I can't figure the motive. If we're forced to shut down, who would benefit from it? Certainly not the employees."

Ashley spoke thoughtfully. "Who *would* benefit if you were shut down?"

Jeanine returned to the room and volunteered, "Well, Tysinger probably wouldn't benefit from it, but he would certainly be glad to hear that we lost our business."

As a result of their report, Tysinger had been indicted along with several others and was awaiting trial for taking bribes to protect the marijuana growers. The investigation had uncovered several million dollars worth of marijuana.

"Could Tysinger be behind something like this, Ashley?" Jeanine asked.

"If he is, it would be tough to prove. I'm sure he wouldn't allow himself to be directly involved."

Rafe mentioned a possibility. "It might be worth checking out the activities of that guy Tysinger sent to get Rafe—you remember, Pete Wilson. What do you think?"

"I think any idea is worth pursuing at this point," Ashley responded. "The hearing is set for this coming Friday. We don't have much time."

"Will you be here on Friday, Rafe?" Raul's question was one Ashley had wanted to ask, but she wasn't sure she wanted to hear the answer.

Rafe sat there for a moment, mentally reviewing his schedule. "There's a possibility I could get away Thursday night, but I'd have to turn around and go back on Saturday." He looked over at Ashley with a question in his eyes. She smiled her response. Whenever he could make it would be fine. "I've never seen Ashley in action. This should prove interesting."

Ashley overslept the next morning, having forgotten to set her alarm. If Tasha hadn't awakened her by sitting on her chest and licking her nose, she might have spent the day asleep.

My hectic weeks and sleepless weekends are beginning to catch up with me, she decided, as she forced herself out of bed and under the shower. She smiled as she remembered that she and Rafe had managed to get some sleep over the weekend, but at rather odd hours. By the time she arrived in the kitchen, Rafe had coffee made and was carrying on one of his many conversations with Tasha, who sat on a chair next to him and listened while he kept an eye on the frying bacon.

Without a word Ashley padded over, sat down on his lap, and buried her head in his neck. He smelled so good. His aftershave lotion should be banned from the market, she thought. It was alluring enough to create riots. Rafe took the opportunity to kiss her exposed neck, which caused chills to run down her body. They smelled the burning bacon at the same time. Rafe jumped to his feet, almost causing Ashley to fall flat on her bottom. As she scrambled to get her balance, he attempted to rescue their breakfast.

"I wish you'd warn me when you're going to make sudden moves like that," she complained.

He was busy placing fresh strips of bacon in the skillet and gave her a brief glance over his shoulder. "Sorry, I seem to be out of practice on how to treat a woman." His grin contradicted the serious tone of voice.

She decided to ignore the comment and began to prepare orange juice and toast. She tried not to cling to him when he was ready to leave, and her only comfort was the work waiting for her when he was gone. She hoped he would be able to make it back on Thursday. As the days went by Ashley had the same thought more than once.

The investigator's supplemental report on James Jackson turned up some interesting news about his son that Ashley thought might be the clue they were looking for, but it was a long shot. As the week progressed, it became obvious to her that it was the only chance they had. If she could prove in court that the suit had been filed in order to strike back at the McCords, she had a good chance of getting the case dismissed. Unfortunately, the burden of proof for the allegation fell on her. The only way she could prove it would be to get Jackson on the stand and force him to admit that he had deliberately caused the spill. Could she do it? Would the judge allow it? Would opposing counsel stand for it? She didn't know, but she could see no other way to win Raul the time needed to fulfill his company's contracts.

At that point in her hectic week, Ashley received a phone call that wiped all thoughts of her profession from her mind. Her doctor's office was calling to report on the tests they'd run the week before. "Your test was positive," a nurse told her cheerfully. "You're pregnant."

Ashley replaced the phone in a state of shock. Pregnant. Of course they had done nothing to prevent it from happening, but somehow she hadn't expected it. Once more she wished for Rafe's presence. This was one piece of news she couldn't tell him over the phone. They had never discussed a family, but she knew he would make an excellent father. It was herself that she was unsure of. What did she know about babies? Could she cope with a family and a career? She really needed Rafe's comforting at the moment.

When the phone rang the second time, Ashley felt immune to any further shocks.

It was Ralph Begley and he wanted to see her. Mystified—she hadn't talked with him since their meeting months before—she waited to hear what was on his mind. It wasn't long in coming.

"I understand that you agreed to represent a new client for us: McCord Industries?"

Puzzled, Ashley replied, "That's right, sir. They were served with papers last week and asked me to represent them."

"I see." Begley sat back in his large overstuffed chair, his fingers drumming on the arm. "Isn't that your husband's name?"

"Yes, sir." She smiled pleasantly.

"Does he hold some interest in the company?" Begley's eyes were cold.

"No, he doesn't. The firm is owned and operated by Raul McCord, my husband's brother." She waited, knowing he'd get to the purpose of his questions sooner or later.

A sigh escaped Begley, and his jaw seemed to set. "You know, Ashley, I recognize that you're a relative newcomer to this area." He paused, making sure he had her undivided attention. "Maybe you aren't aware of just how high feelings run against these big companies that have pushed their way into our area from California. It's not enough that they've destroyed the air and water down there so nobody can live in it." Once again he paused as though keeping a tight rein on his emotions. "Now they're trying to turn Oregon into the same kind of wasteland." His look dared Ashley to refute his statements.

She sat quietly, waiting for him to continue.

"Our firm has been very careful not to support any particular faction involved in the environmental dispute. We have to be nonpartisan. We're here to provide a service to our clients, but we, ourselves, don't take sides. But then, you already know that, don't you?"

"Yes, sir."

He leaned forward in his chair, his expression hard.

"I don't want you handling this case."

A tiny gasp escaped from Ashley. "Mr. Begley, the hearing is set to take place in two days."

"Yes, well, I want you to tell McCord you can't represent him, that this firm cannot represent him." His statement rang with finality.

"But what reason can I possibly give for doing that, sir?" she asked.

"Conflict of interest."

"What conflict of interest, Mr. Begley?"

Astonishment rolled across Begley's face like a cloud crossing the sun. Nobody argued with this man, not members of the firm, anyway. "I just explained to you, Ashley. We do not represent any California companies that move up here and pollute our air and water supplies."

"Mr. Begley, sir... In the first place, no one has proved that that's what McCord Industries is doing. After going into all the facts during the past few days, I have found no evidence to support the charges against them. There has been only one incident of contamination since they opened, and I don't think it was an accident.''

"Fine. Then let someone else represent them. They shouldn't have any trouble finding legal representation elsewhere.''

"But, Mr. Begley," she implored, "I've already accepted the case and prepared for it. No one else could possibly give adequate representation with less than two days to prepare." She could not believe that he would close his mind to the ethical considerations involved in suddenly refusing to represent a client without adequate cause.

Begley's expression pinned Ashley to her chair much like a butterfly to a board. "You are too closely involved to give objective counseling. You should never have accepted the case in the first place." He glanced at his watch. "I have an appointment now, Ashley. I'm afraid I don't have time for further discussion.''

Ashley nodded and stood up, staring at Ralph Begley as though she'd never seen him before. She had her orders. It was up to her to carry them out.

Chapter Nine

By the time Ashley reached her office she was shaking so much she could barely stand. Withdraw from the case. How simple that sounded. Such an easy command to make, but how could she drop Raul's case two days before trial? Her integrity was at stake.

She needed to get away, to come to grips with the pain she was feeling. Thank God she'd kept her afternoon clear of appointments.

Ashley escaped from the office and drove to Washington Park. Perched high on one of the western hills, the park directly overlooked Portland. Its rose garden was one of her favorite places in the city.

Although the air was cool there was no wind, and she found the garden deserted.

She wandered through the roses and finally settled on a bench that gave a clear view of the city. Images from the past began to drift across her mind. She remembered her father's shock when she first informed him that she wanted to become a lawyer and her mother's quiet support of Ashley's desire to go out in the world. She remembered the hours of study during her pre-law courses, the grueling hours spent in law school, and her single-minded efforts to build a career during the last five years. How ironic that the career she sought to save by a hasty marriage now threatened that same marriage.

Ashley had reached a point in her life when she had to make a choice. The news of her pregnancy caused an upsurge of unfamiliar feelings. She had never given much thought to having a family. If she had, she would have pictured herself in the role her mother had chosen, but Rafe had taught her so much about relationships. She and Rafe were entirely different from her own parents, and in her heart Ashley knew that she could depend on Rafe's loving support to help raise their child. Now that the shock had worn off, she was becoming excited about her pregnancy, wondering whether she would have a miniature Rafe, knowing she would love his child.

Over the months, Ashley's life had moved into a new dimension of love and fulfillment. Rafe had given her so much and had asked for so little in return.

She also acknowledged that, regardless of who a client was, she could not in clear conscience refuse to represent that client so close to the date of the hearing. It was not fair to the client or to the attorney who would attempt to replace her. Her professional integrity was now on the line.

As she began to weigh her options she knew she had no choice, professionally or personally. Ralph Begley had delivered his ultimatum. By ignoring it, she knew she forfeited all chances of being made a partner. Her very job would be at stake.

A cool breeze finally interrupted Ashley's concentration, and she realized she'd been sitting in one position for hours. It was time to go home. The phone was ringing when she walked into her house. Throwing her coat and purse at a chair, she grabbed the receiver.

"Hello?" she said in a breathless voice.

"Ashley? What's wrong?" Rafe sounded so close that he could have been in the next room. Oh, how she wished he were. Unexpected tears flowed. She bit her lip, trying to regain control of herself.

"Nothing's wrong, Rafe. I just rushed to get the phone." Her voice had a definite wobble in it, but perhaps he would attribute the sound to the long-distance line.

"I thought I'd let you know I'm going to be able to manage that quick trip to Oregon. Can you pick me up at the airport Thursday night at nine?"

"You know better than to ask that question. You'll recognize me when you get off the plane. I'll be the one doing handsprings along the concourse."

He was still laughing when they hung up. Rafe was coming. Life suddenly looked a great deal brighter. She wasn't sure how she'd broach the subject of her pregnancy. Perhaps she would wait until the hearing was behind her. She might have to tell him she was not only pregnant but metaphorically barefoot, or at least unemployed. She was already recovering from the shock of Begley's demand and realized she wasn't as upset as she would have been a year earlier. Begley, Henderson & Howe wasn't the only law office in town. She had built a reputation that would enable her to find another position. Rafe and the baby were more important concerns in her life at the moment.

She could hardly wait to see Rafe's reaction to the news of the impending arrival.

Flight 287 from San Francisco arrived on time. Ashley felt certain she couldn't have survived the wait much longer. Her face glowing, she watched as each person stepped through the door of the plane.

Rafe's face lit up when he spotted her. When he reached her he pulled her into his arms, kissing her passionately as he crushed her body against his.

She managed to pull away from him, her face flushed and her eyes sparkling. "Rafe—" she glanced around quickly "—everybody's watching! Despite rumor to the contrary, not *every* trial lawyer is an exhibitionist." The look he gave her caused her color to turn a deeper shade of pink. He'd mentally stripped her and made love to her with his eyes. She found him irresistible when he was in this mood, and she had trouble keeping her hands away from him until they could reach the car.

He'd carried one bag on the plane, so they went directly to the car in the parking lot. After throwing the bag in the back, Rafe slid into the front seat next to her and then turned to her. "I don't dare start kissing you here, or we'll get arrested before I finish."

She leaned over and kissed him on the cheek. "There. Hopefully that will hold you until we get home." She batted her eyelashes with coy bashfulness.

"Not very likely, but I'll try to contain myself."

As Rafe found change to pay the parking fee, Ashley managed to move a little closer to him and rested her hand on his thigh. She could feel his muscles flex while he tried to ignore her. She didn't help matters by stroking his leg with a feather touch.

"Enough!" he growled as he grabbed her hand. He moved it back to her lap, where his hand lingered, finding that he had access to various areas belonging to Ashley.

"Not fair, Rafe," she remonstrated as she wriggled in her seat.

"I'm glad to know you agree with me. Now behave yourself." He flashed her a smile that reminded her of why she'd married him in the first place. *They were worse than a couple of teenagers who couldn't keep their hands away from each other.* Ashley grinned at the thought. Somehow she had missed that part of growing up, but she was glad she had waited to share it with Rafe.

Tasha greeted them at the door and, when she saw Rafe, marched over to him and welcomed him with a purr and a soft caress of her back against his leg. Tasha never did that to anyone, not even Ashley.

"I don't believe this. What have you done to my cat?"

He carried his bag into the bedroom. "I haven't done anything."

Ashley watched as Tasha followed him into the room and jumped onto his suitcase. He reached down and massaged behind her ears and under her chin. "She's just being sociable."

"I find it disgusting. Why, she's practically slobbering all over you."

He grinned. "Yes, she is, isn't she?"

"You insufferable egotist." She grabbed him around his neck, pulling herself up so that her mouth could meet his. She put all the endless longing she'd felt since he'd left three days before into her kiss. He was most cooperative in returning her offering. At last Ashley managed to pull away from him and rubbed her head under his chin. "I'm forced to admit that I admire her taste," she said with a defeated sigh.

Rafe had eaten on the plane, so they wasted no time in going to bed. As Rafe pulled her into his arms, he asked, "Should I call Raul and let him know I'm here?"

"I told him you would be. He seemed relieved." They lay there in contented silence for a moment; then Rafe whispered, "Are you going to sleep?" The soft words tickled her ear.

"Not very likely, with you lying next to me in 'that' condition," she pointed out as her hand gently touched him.

"I can't tell from that comment whether you're bragging or complaining." His tongue touched her ear, causing her to shiver.

She moved so that she was above him, her hair falling around her shoulders and brushing against his chest. She began to kiss him just under his jaw—soft little kisses that caused the surface of his skin to quiver. She moved down his chest, kissing first one nipple, which hardened as she lingered to stroke it with her tongue, then moving lazily across his broad chest to the other one.

Rafe's groan was music to her ears. Between her hair brushing against his sensitive skin and her mouth and tongue touching him with delicate skill, his body began to tremble. So much for bragging or complaining. Her tongue darted along his ribs, tracing them faithfully, then it paused for further exploration around his navel.

"Ashley!" Rafe's hands came up and encircled her waist. He lifted her so that her hips came down upon him in perfect symmetry. She could feel the tremor through him as their bodies and spirits intermingled in an embrace, forming a unity and a communion.

She began to move on him, accelerating the pace until both of them became caught up in the rhythm and flow of their lovemaking. His hands reached to restrain her abandoned movements, but it was too late—the force of their tempestuous pace swept them both far out from shore, and the frenzied and frantic feeling of moments before rolled and tossed them on sensuous waves, until they once again were washed up on the shore of fulfillment.

* * *

Both were damp from their loving exertions, and Ashley's hair clung to her brow and across one cheek. Rafe clutched her in his arms, reluctant to allow her to pull away from him in this moment of total sharing and undiminished joy. Never had she responded to him with such openness and abandonment.

Rafe could feel her heart fluttering like a bird captured and afraid. He began to soothe her overheated body with his hand, easing down the length of her back and up over her derriere. Ashley had become the focal point of his existence—his love was almost frightening in its intensity. He drifted off to sleep, a smile hovering on his face.

When Rafe's eyes opened it was daylight, and Ashley stood by the bed watching him. He was startled to find her dressed and ready to leave. She bent over the bed and kissed him.

"I've got to go, love. There's coffee and fresh orange juice made." She smiled as she witnessed his bewilderment. "I need to get to the office early—there's so much to be done." She cocked her head. "You know, I rather like to see you asleep in my bed. It's seldom I'm ever awake before you," she added with an impish grin.

Turning to go, she paused. "The hearing starts at ten, so if I don't see you before—" she gave a half salute "—I'll see you in court."

Rafe looked at the clock by the bed. Seven-thirty. He hadn't heard the alarm or felt her stir—he'd been more tired than he realized. Maybe it had something to do with coming home to relax. He didn't sleep as well any more in his comfortable condominium in San Francisco, although he'd been quite pleased with all it had to offer until he met Ashley. She'd managed to ruin his sleeping habits as well as disturb the even tenor of his bachelor existence. She had a lot to answer for, that woman!

He felt a movement on the bed and watched Tasha as she picked her way across to the pillow Ashley had deserted.

"I'm sorry, Tash, ole girl, you'll never be able to take her place, but I suppose you can stay." The cat gave him a lazy stare, then sat down and proceeded to bathe. "You're not easily intimidated, are you?" His rhetorical question remained unanswered as he headed for the shower.

Around nine-thirty Ashley developed an unexpected case of nerves, a problem she'd overcome early in her career. But then this case wasn't typical. And she wasn't at all confident that she could win it.

It would be bad enough to lose her job; to lose the hearing as well would be a double blow.

She was glad of the interruption when her secretary buzzed to say that Raul had arrived. As they walked to the courthouse he teased Ashley about Rafe using the hearing as an excuse to come back to see her.

"He doesn't need an excuse, you idiot," she said, laughing at the idea.

"He says he's afraid you'll get tired of him hanging around all the time if he visits too frequently." He shook his head. "I've never known Rafe to be as unsure of himself as he is with you. A lesser man would probably be intimidated."

"Now that I will never believe." She smiled up at the man walking alongside her. "You won't ever convince me that Rafe doesn't recognize his own worth."

They made their way through the echoing halls of the marble courthouse and entered the empty courtroom. Ashley wasn't surprised—they were a few minutes early.

The opposing counsel appeared and, nodding to Ashley, began to lay his papers out on the desk. She and Raul moved to the defense table and she began to arrange her papers for presentation. Neither attorney had requested a jury trial, and there were no visitors to the courtroom. Ashley kept glancing over her shoulder, watching for Rafe. He had not yet arrived when the bailiff stepped into the room from the judge's chambers and announced, "All rise as the Multnomah County Circuit Court is called to order, the Honorable Jed Downing presiding."

With no fanfare and in a steady voice, the plaintiff's attorney presented his client's case to the judge. The man knew what he was doing. He had constructed a tight case from circumstantial evidence. She had to convince the judge there were other, more reasonable ways to view the issue.

The plaintiff's attorney presented dates, figures, and diagrams that, according to him, proved the case against McCord Industries. Then he called several witnesses who were employees of the company. Ashley noted their restlessness on the stand and their uneasiness whenever they were forced to answer questions they were afraid were harmful to the company. With each witness she limited her cross-examination to how they felt about working at the plant. Did they feel it was safe? Did they consider the way in which waste materials were handled a hazard? She waited for Jackson to be called as a witness and was not disappointed.

Jackson appeared to be in his late forties. He was a tall, stoop-shouldered man with a receding hairline. He sat quietly in the witness chair, his eyes trained on the plaintiff's attorney.

When her turn came to cross-examine, Ashley took her time approaching the witness. After the opposing attorney had sat down, Jackson seemed to have trouble knowing what to do with his hands. His demeanor was similar to that of a penitent schoolboy having to face the principal.

At that point, Rafe entered the courtroom and slipped into the last row of visitors' chairs, but Ashley was unaware of his arrival. Rafe recognized Jackson, having seen him at the plant, but the man had aged considerably since then. A likable man, but at the moment he appeared ill at ease. Rafe didn't imagine anyone would feel comfortable on the witness stand, regardless of the person's guilt or innocence. He found the courtroom atmosphere stifling.

Ashley proceeded with her cross-examination as Rafe sat back to watch.

"Mr. Jackson." Ashley spoke in a low, clear voice. "You have stated that you were in charge of the production line at the time the spill in question took place, is that correct?"

His eyes flickered to the other attorney, then to her. "Yes." His answer was scarcely audible.

The judge leaned forward from his position above the witness. "You will have to speak up, Mr. Jackson, so that the court reporter can hear you." The judge gave the witness a reassuring smile.

Jackson cleared his throat and nodded. Raising his voice, he repeated: "Yes."

"Who besides yourself had authority to enter the area where the spill occurred, Mr. Jackson?"

He mumbled an answer.

The judge spoke once again. "Mr. Jackson, you must speak up. None of us can hear you." His voice was not quite as pleasant as it had been.

"The two floor supervisors."

"I see." Ashley paused, wondering how to get the next question answered without opposing counsel raising an objection.

"How well do you know Pete Wilson, Mr. Jackson?" She watched as the color faded from Jackson's face, leaving him parchment white. Whether he answered the question or not, she knew she had him!

"Objection, Your Honor. The question is irrelevant to the proceedings."

The judge eyed Ashley. "Does Pete Wilson have some connection to the spill being discussed, Ms. Allison?"

"It is my strong belief that he does, sir." The opposing counsel looked bewildered, and she knew the Department of Environmental Quality had no idea what was involved in the case.

"Objection overruled. The witness may answer the question," the judge stated.

Jackson looked ill; his skin had turned a pasty color. Perspiration dotted his forehead. He looked at the other attorney, then back to Ashley. With head bowed and shoulders slumped, he said, "I hardly know him at all."

"But he knew about your son, didn't he, Mr. Jackson?"

"Objection, Your Honor," came from the other attorney. "This is the most irregular line of questioning I've ever witnessed in a courtroom."

"Ms. Allison," the judge stated in a weary tone, "I hardly see that Mr. Jackson's son has anything to do with the matter presented for hearing today. What is your point?"

"My point, Your Honor, is that I believe Mr. Jackson knows more about the spill than he has admitted. I believe that he can explain why it happened and that his involvement is the result of pressure brought to bear on him. I believe Mr. Jackson's actions on the day of the spill are directly related to an attempt to protect his son."

The other attorney watched Ashley with amazement. When he could speak, he said, "Your Honor, I believe Ms. Allison is the victim of too much late-night television, sir. That has to be the most ridiculous plot anyone could have dreamed up. Creative, perhaps, but it has no place in a court of law."

The judge sat with bowed head for a moment, then nodded. "Continue with your cross-examination."

Ashley felt relief seeping through her system. One hurdle passed. Now, if she could get the answers she needed . . . She returned to the witness. "Mr. Jackson, is your twenty-five-year-old son presently employed?"

"Yes."

"Where?"

"The Port of Portland."

"When your son filled out his job application at the Port of Portland, did he report his drug conviction on the application?"

Jackson paled. She knew he had tried to protect his son, but at the expense of McCord Industries. She felt sorry for him, but her feelings did not stop her from trying to get the information she needed. "No."

"If the Port knew about the false application, he'd lose his job, wouldn't he, Mr. Jackson?"

"Yes." Once again his answers were almost inaudible but, because of the silence in the courtroom, his words rang out clearly.

In a very gentle tone Ashley asked, "What did Pete Wilson say to you, Mr. Jackson, when he approached you about causing an accident in the plant?"

"Objection, Your Honor!" The opposing counsel's face glowed with anger. "Counsel is leading the witness. There is absolutely no evidence in this hearing that anyone approached anyone to cause the spill in question."

"Sustained. Please rephrase the question."

"What did Pete Wilson say to you when he first approached you, Mr. Jackson?"

"He said he knew my son had straightened himself out. He knew he was married and they were expecting a baby, and he was sure I wouldn't want to see him lose his new position."

"That was all?"

He looked at her with something like pity at her naive question.

"That was enough."

"What did you do to cause the spill, Mr. Jackson?"

In a trembling voice, Jackson told the court that he had slipped into the production area and wedged a piece of wood in one of the ducts that drained waste chemicals, knowing the flow would hit the wood and begin to splash over the drain. By the time anyone noticed, the chemicals were pouring onto the floor and draining away through the outside doorways. The spill succeeded in reaching the Sandy River, contaminating it; the incident was immediately reported to the Department of Environmental Quality.

"Did Mr. Wilson tell you why he wanted you to cause the spill?"

"No. I didn't ask."

"Thank you, Mr. Jackson." She looked at the judge. "No further questions, Your Honor."

The judge nodded. "The witness is excused."

The plaintiff's counsel approached the bench. "Your Honor, the Department of Environmental Quality does not use intimidation, blackmail, or other coercion to get evidence of the nature presented in this law suit." He paused and glanced at the defense table where Ashley and Raul sat, then back to the judge. "We have more reports of violations each day than we can possibly investigate. We are not out to persecute, Your Honor; we're here to protect."

He walked to his table, picked up some papers, and walked back to the bench. "The exhibit that has been entered into the record states on its face that McCord Industries has not met the standards set to contain and control contaminating waste products. I feel we have proven that today. No one has denied the spill in question. The contaminants that polluted the Sandy River destroyed fish, polluted the water supply of a rather large area, and caused injury to undetermined numbers of wildlife and game.

As stated in my motion, I believe McCord Industries should be shut down immediately, and upon trial of this matter, we will prove that the plant constitutes a threat to its environmental surroundings and should be closed on a permanent basis." He moved to his table and sat down.

Ashley approached the bench. "Your Honor, I believe there has been enough testimony to show a preponderance of evidence that one violation of murky origin is not sufficient reason to warrant closing the McCord Industries plant, either on a temporary or on a permanent basis. We respectfully request that the motion be denied and the case dismissed." Ashley returned to her chair.

The judge spoke to the plaintiff's counsel. "Am I correct in assuming that you have no evidence that might support your allegations that McCord Industries is hazardous to the environment other than the one incident discussed today?"

"That's correct, sir."

"In that case I see no reason to prolong a decision on this matter. I find for the defendant. Case dismissed."

The judge stood as the bailiff intoned, "All rise. The Multnomah County Circuit Court, the Honorable Jed Downing presiding, is dismissed."

Raul turned around and grabbed Ashley in a bear hug. "You did it! You cleared us! You were fantastic!"

Ashley blushed at Raul's affectionate enthusiasm but shared his relief that matters had turned out so well. Raul added, "I've got to call Jeanine and tell her the news. I'll talk to you later." She watched him rush down the aisle—and spotted Rafe. He was sitting in the back row next to the door, but Raul dashed by without noticing him. Ashley made quick work of placing papers back in her briefcase and hurried to Rafe, who stood at her approach.

"I didn't see you come in, Rafe. I'm glad you made it. Did you see the whole hearing?"

Rafe's face masked his thoughts. "I came in just as Jackson took the stand." He paused, an inscrutable expression in his eyes. "Congratulations."

"Is something wrong, Rafe?"

"Wrong? Of course not. You won your case, and as far as I can judge, you did an excellent job." Ashley could not tell anything from his expression. Whatever he thought, she wasn't going to find out now. She took his arm and started out the door. "Do you want to get a bite to eat?" Ashley led the way to the stairway and started down the steps; Rafe kept pace with her.

"I can't. I have to call California as soon as I get back to the house. I had to cut a call short or I wouldn't have made it when I did." He stopped as they reached the sidewalk. "I'll see you when you get home."

Ashley found it difficult to respond in a natural voice. "Fine, I shouldn't be late." She watched him stride down the street as though eager to leave. *Don't be silly,* she admonished herself. *Just because he didn't grab you and kiss you passionately the way he did at the airport, you think your marriage is failing!*

She discovered that her instincts had been right when she arrived home. Rafe was waiting in the living room, his bag sitting near the door.

"I thought you weren't leaving until the morning."

"I had to change my reservations. We've called an emergency meeting first thing tomorrow. I need to be there." He stood across the room from her, his body tense.

"It's more than a sudden business meeting, isn't it, Rafe?" she asked softly.

He looked at her as though he'd never seen her before, as though he was seeing a stranger who didn't impress him. Finally he answered, "Yes." He moved to the window and looked out, and she waited. A fluttering had begun in her stomach. "I've been thinking all afternoon about how slim the chances were that I'd ever see you in action, but the fact remains that I have."

"And?"

"And today, watching you excel in your profession, I realized that I don't even know the woman I married. It's quite possible that the woman I thought I married exists only in my imagination." He turned away from the window and moved back to her, studying her intently.

Ashley shook her head in confusion. "I'm afraid I don't understand."

He continued to study her. "It hit me today, Ashley, what it means—your being an attorney—a highly skilled trial lawyer with all the necessary killer instincts. I can understand your success—you go straight for the jugular."

The words he spoke spilled out into the quiet room and bounced around her. Ashley heard the sounds but had difficulty absorbing their meaning. Rafe continued to speak as though thinking aloud. "When I first met you I saw an attractive woman who stirred me as no other woman I'd ever met had, and I wanted you. I took unfair advantage of your lack of experience and caused you to want me." He moved toward her as though to touch her, then dropped his hand. "I had no concept of what the other part of you was like until today. I sat there and watched you, wondering what it would be like to have those skills turned against me. For a moment the thought shook me." His gaze wandered over her face and he frowned, noticing her lack of color for the first time.

Moving to the door, he leaned over and picked up his bag. "I'm hurting you, and God knows I don't want to do that. I think I'd better leave before I say any more."

She was surprised at how calm she sounded as she asked, "Would you like me to take you to the airport?"

He hesitated, glancing at his watch. "I'm afraid I've left it a little late to call a cab. Would you mind?" How polite he sounded.

"No. I had planned to, anyway."

Rafe drove. They were almost to the airport when he spoke.

"Ashley, I've got a lot of thinking to do, and I need some time. I've been driving myself—" he paused "—just as you have. I can see what it's doing to us. You shouldn't have to justify who and what you are to me. It's just that I'm not sure I can accept who you are at the moment."

"Do you want a divorce?"

"No!" Then he qualified the statement. "At least, not necessarily. I'm just facing the fact that marriage means more than legalizing our right to make love. I thought we had a similar value system, a similar outlook—"

"When did you decide that we don't?"

His face reflected the agony his thoughts were causing him as he pulled up in front of the airport. "When I saw you tear apart a man whose folly was in attempting to protect his son. Why, Ashley?" He was almost pleading. "Why was it so important to the case? Couldn't you have made the same point without dragging that poor man's most private pain out for everyone to see?"

"Rafe, I conducted the case in the only way I could, if I wanted to win it." Her gaze remained steady. "I think you'd better catch your plane." One part of her noted his face go pale at her unemotional tone, and anguish showed in the blue depths of his eyes.

He got out of the car, and she moved over and looked at him for a moment through the open window. "Goodbye, Rafe." She then released the hand brake and drove off, refusing to glance into her rearview mirror. The pain began to grow and spread through her body like flood water inching across a dam. "I mustn't think of him right now." Her voice sounded loud in the quiet car. "Think of other things, Ashley. You won the case. That was the important thing. You mustn't lose sight of your priorities. At least Raul was pleased with the outcome." She knew she'd done the only thing she could. "I wonder if winning will justify my ignoring Begley's orders."

Ashley knew that an attorney never entered a courtroom to lose, not if that attorney wanted a career as a trial attorney. She'd never faced how painful winning could be.

Chapter Ten

Ashley returned home. The house had never seemed so empty. She sat down on the sofa and stared into the cold fireplace, remembering the plans she'd made for the evening. She'd intended to prepare the only casserole she'd ever learned to make. The wine waited in the refrigerator. That, along with the candlelight and a small fire in the fireplace were to help set the mood for her news. Her sudden choked laugh sounded more like a sob.

Not telling him doesn't make him less a father, she reminded herself, *but for some reason I don't think the news would have helped matters tonight.* The awful thing, the thought that kept eating away at her, was that she couldn't blame Rafe for his reaction.

Knowing his attitude toward attorneys, she should have been better prepared for it. As he had pointed out, he might never have seen her in a courtroom. With her career as uncertain as it was at the moment, and the added advent of motherhood, Ashley might have managed to practice on a limited basis and been the woman Rafe thought she was.

He was right. She wasn't that woman, but he'd made the woman he saw come alive within her, to begin to have meaning and substance to Ashley so that she wanted to become that warm, loving creature. She wanted to develop the emotional and loving side of her nature that had lain dormant within her.

Ashley began to notice the chill in the room. As she stood up, Tasha reminded her that she hadn't been fed but for once didn't make a federal case out of it. She followed Ashley into the kitchen and waited patiently for her meal. Rafe had even managed to transform Tasha.

As she climbed into bed, Ashley admitted to herself that she had reason to be exhausted. Her pregnancy notwithstanding, she'd had a traumatic day. Word would have reached Begley that Ashley had not withdrawn from representing McCord Industries. He would probably consider her win a final insult to his authority.

At long last her body's needs overcame her and she fell into a restless sleep, the scent of cedar haunting her dreams.

Ashley managed to retain a blessed feeling of numbness during the next few weeks. She waited for some word from Begley, but heard nothing.

One day at the office, when she'd been involved in depositions and had escaped to the restroom, she returned to hear a conversation between one of the attorneys of her firm and one of the opposing attorneys there for the depositions. She heard her name mentioned and paused. The opposing attorney was saying, "My God, Fred, that woman was a barracuda in depositions today. I've seen some aggressive women lawyers, but Allison is something else."

She waited, unsure of how to get past the door to the conference room without being seen when she heard the reply. "Oh, don't mind her, Jim. You know how these women lawyers are. They think they have to look tougher, act meaner, and hit harder than any man. She's a good lawyer, though. We're pleased to have her in the firm."

Their voices faded as they left the room through another door. She went into her office, ostensibly to check phone messages but in reality to regain her composure. Was that how others saw her? She'd been too busy learning how to practice law to be concerned about her image. She tried to shrug off the comments. They weren't all bad—more like backhanded compliments. It was good to hear that at least one member of the firm considered her an asset.

The following morning she woke up sobbing. Her dream still floated in her mind like a shroud. She'd been with Rafe and it was just like the first time she had awakened and found him kissing her. She'd been holding him close, stroking his face and shoulders, when in the dream he became Virgil Tysinger. He was saying, "So you're a lawyer, huh? You really know how to pick the barracudas, Rafe." She'd glanced behind her and saw Rafe standing there watching her, a look of disgust and distaste on his face. Her sobbing had followed her out of the dream and she woke up, facing the loneliness of her life. She cried until she was limp. Then she lay exhausted, her chest hurting from the great gulps of air she'd taken in an attempt to quell the dry sobs.

One morning in late November Ashley received an interoffice envelope marked "Confidential"—which could only mean its contents concerned an administrative matter. The wheels of justice might turn exceedingly slow, but she knew they'd caught up with her. The message was a request that Ashley attend a partners' meeting scheduled for the following Tuesday at five-thirty.

Ashley arrived on time but was the last one to come into the room. She glanced around the conference table at the eleven men. *I wonder if this is how a condemned criminal feels,* she thought as they watched her take a seat. She placed her hands loosely in her lap and waited.

Ralph Begley spoke. "Thank you for joining us today, Ashley." He refused to meet her eyes, a sure sign that his news wasn't pleasant. "There are some matters we wish to discuss with you. We've been going over your record." He paused, looking down at his notes as if to confirm his facts. "Five years now, isn't it?"

Ashley nodded.

"We've been quite pleased with your contribution to the firm, Ashley."

Then why can't you look me in the eye when you speak to me? she wondered.

"You've been honest and straightforward with us," Begley continued, "and we've tried to work with you on the same level." He paused, then cleared his throat. He glanced around at the other men seated at the table. "A few weeks ago I had occasion to speak to you on a matter regarding what I felt to be a conflict of interest within our firm."

Ashley wondered why he was prolonging the meeting. Perhaps he derived some sort of pleasure from pointing out to his more liberal partners that he had been right in his reluctance to hire a woman attorney. *I've probably set the cause of hiring female attorneys in this firm back fifty years.* She mentally apologized to any would-be successors who would not understand the reason for their rejection.

"At that time—" Begley's voice began to sound hoarse as though he had to force his speech "—I strongly advised Ashley to turn her case over to someone else."

"Advised"? "Ordered" would be more accurate. She waited with no expression on her face.

"She did not do so."

Eleven pairs of eyes turned on Ashley as she sat there.

You would think I'd stolen the key to the executive men's room.

"Our firm has never been faced with a situation quite like this one, and we've spent several weeks discussing what, if anything, should be done."

Ashley forced herself to meet his eyes, but he was having trouble sustaining the contact.

"Out of the several meetings that have been held regarding this issue, one point seems to remain outstanding. To be a part of the firm, it is necessary that each of us recognize the team effort it takes to make the firm successful. If we each start pulling in a different direction, we'll never move forward."

All right. The verdict was in—and she was out.

Begley paused and poured himself a glass of water from the decanter at his elbow. She was surprised to see how difficult he was finding it to tell her she was fired. She had an insane desire to do it for him, but she managed to restrain herself.

"Ashley." He paused, then cleared his throat. "It is my rather unpleasant task to inform you that in a unanimous vote the partnership has decided to request that you seek employment elsewhere."

There, that wasn't so bad, was it? She wanted to console him, then forced herself to face the fact that she'd just been fired from her first and only position as a lawyer. *Is this how shock feels?* She felt so differently than she had when Rafe left, perhaps because she'd already come to terms with this eventuality. At the moment all she could feel was a sense of relief that something definite had taken place. Now she could pick up the pieces and go on with her life.

All eyes were trained on her, and she realized with a start that they were waiting for her to say something. *Like what? Oh well, here goes....*

"Thank you, Mr. Begley, for taking the time to explain your position. I was aware at the time I made the decision to attend the hearing that there was a possibility my employment with the firm would be terminated.'' She glanced around the table with a pleasant smile. ''I can't say that I'm surprised, because I'm not. I'm very sorry that the situation arose, but I would be less than honest if I didn't tell you that given the same set of circumstances, and knowing what I know now—'' her smile grew ''—I would make exactly the same decision,'' she finished in a soft, firm voice.

Glancing back at Begley, she asked, ''When would you like me to leave?''

The men continued to stare at her with varying degrees of puzzlement, and she realized that none of them had expected her reaction. *They probably expected tears and hysteria. Well, sorry to disappoint you, fellas, but if I didn't do that when I was kidnapped, you won't catch me doing it over a job.*

''There's no rush, of course,'' Begley said to reassure her—unnecessarily, as it happened. Her savings account and severance pay would see her through several months, if not a couple of years. She wouldn't be without work that long, she knew. ''We would appreciate your handling any cases pending during the next four or five weeks. As for the rest, if you could work with the other attorneys so that they can pick up from there, it should make the transition easier for the clients involved.''

She nodded. ''Of course. Then the end of the year would probably be a suitable time for me to leave.''

"Oh, it doesn't have to be that soon, Ashley. If you'd like to stay on until, say, March or so, that's perfectly satisfactory with us."

Once again she smiled, finding it hard to hide her amusement. She was still refusing to play by the old school rules the men seemed to understand so well. "My January calendar is almost empty, as I had intended to take some time off and spend a few weeks in California with my husband." No one knew that those plans had been abandoned some time ago. She had continued to keep the time open, knowing that she would need a break from her work at the office.

In the end, it was very simple to start severing her ties with the office, and she found herself looking forward to the first break in her routine since she had left law school. She needed some time to herself.

During the week between Christmas and New Year's an ice storm hit Portland, paralyzing traffic and causing most people to stay home. Eager to finish clearing out her desk, Ashley chose to leave her car at home and walk to work. Her boots had nonskid soles that made it easy enough to walk, and the exercise was welcome.

She took a shortcut to save time and distance and marveled at the beauty of the ice-weighted trees. Portland had become an artist's paradise, but the damage to utility lines created chaos for the crews in charge of them. Her office building had escaped the loss of electricity, for which Ashley was thankful after hiking that far.

Once she was in her office, her day became predictable; by the time she was ready to leave, each pending file had full notations of what had been done and what still needed to be done to prepare for trial. She left content with the work she'd accomplished.

The transit mall appeared deserted as Ashley stepped out of the building. The winter light had faded, and she was glad she had decided to leave a little early. She was watching where she walked and didn't notice anyone until a hand touched her arm. She jumped, startled, and glanced up. Rafe stood there, his heavy coat adding to his size. The collar was turned up to protect his neck and ears. No cap covered his thick, wind-ruffled hair. It fell across his forehead in a familiar fashion. Ashley felt as though someone had squeezed her heart. She raised her frightened face to meet Rafe's gaze.

"I'm sorry I startled you, Ashley. I was just on my way upstairs to try to see you." She continued to stare at him, watching his lips as though he were a puppet mouthing words. His face looked as though he'd forgotten how to smile. "I'm glad I didn't miss you."

Trying to regain some self-control, she attempted to joke. "Don't tell me this is another kidnapping attempt?"

She saw the expression in his eyes change as her whimsical response registered. "Is your car here downtown?" he asked.

She shook her head.

"May I give you a ride home?"

Her mouth lifted in an attempt to smile. He sounded so polite, like a little boy properly trained. "That would be very nice, thank you." *You see, I can be polite, too.*

She noted the changes in his face since she'd last seen him. He looked older, much older. She couldn't quite decide why that was. Perhaps "defeated" better described his appearance. He stood there, his broad shoulders slumped, his head not quite erect. His eyes reflected the cold surrounding them.

Rafe led her down the steps and to the street where his car waited by the curb. He had driven to Oregon, hoping he'd make it before the bad weather hit. The roads could be treacherous in the border area between the two states.

They were both silent as he helped her into the car and then hurried around to the driver's side and got in. The car's warmth felt good to Ashley's already chilled legs and feet. Rafe drove with care, taking no chances.

Ashley turned her head toward Rafe, rolling it in a lazy movement against the headrest. Her body felt limp, like a stuffed doll that had suddenly lost all its filling. Her mind was blank; not even fragments of thought interfered with the gray expanse of nothingness.

"How are Raul and Jeanine?"

His eyes flicked to her, then returned to watch the street. "They're fine. I drove up for Christmas. Thank God I managed to miss all of this mess on the road." He was quiet for several moments. "They asked about you."

"Did they? What did you tell them?"

"Very little. They knew something was wrong when you began to refuse their invitations to visit. Raul called me to find out what was going on, and in my usual subtle fashion I told him it was none of his damned business and to butt out." His voice sounded fierce; as was his expression.

Ashley could think of nothing to say, and they lapsed into silence once more. The drive home seemed interminable—tree limbs were down everywhere. City and utility trucks were the only vehicles to be seen except for an occasional Tri-Met Transit bus.

When they parked in front of her house, he helped her out of the car. Then he took the keys from her and opened the door to the house. Tasha greeted them as though they'd left together that morning. She pressed against Rafe's leg as he hung his heavy coat in the hall closet, then followed as he knelt before the fireplace and began to build a fire. Ashley could hear her purr from across the room. At least he knew Tasha was glad to see him. Ashley had no feelings at all at the moment. She hoped she could maintain the numbness until after he left. She wasn't up to discussing divorce arrangements at the moment.

"Would you like some coffee?" she asked in her polite hostess manner.

"That sounds great. Do you have any Kahlua?"

She had started for the kitchen and stopped at his question. "I think so."

"Good. Some of that in the coffee would help to warm us up." The half smile he gave her was well remembered, and she moved away from him and his attractiveness. As she prepared the coffee she hoped Rafe hadn't seen her pain.

By the time she returned to the living room, Rafe had a blazing fire going, had pulled one of the pillows off the couch onto the floor, and lay propped up on the rug before the fire. Tasha was stretched out beside him, still purring. He stood up when she entered the room and took the tray she carried. Ashley had sliced some banana nut bread left over from a weekend spree of baking. He smiled, but made no comment.

"The fire feels good from here. Why don't you join me?" he asked as he settled on the rug and patted the place beside him.

"I think I'd like to change into something more comfortable first." She indicated her suit. Ashley had never seen Rafe in winter clothes and her eyes lingered on the woolen pullover sweater he wore.

Several pieces of the bread were missing when Ashley returned. Since her waistline had begun to spread she'd been forced to purchase some elastic-waisted woolen slacks. Her matching sweater fell in loose folds around her middle, making an effective camouflage.

"Thank you for the ride home," she said matter-of-factly. "I wasn't looking forward to the walk." She sat down beside him and poured herself a cup of coffee. Taking Rafe's advice, she measured a small amount of Kahlua into the steaming cup. She took a small sip and smiled. He was right—it was delicious.

"How did you get to work this morning? Did you ride the bus?" He sounded genuinely interested.

"No, I walked. It really isn't too far if I cut through a couple of parks." They both looked at the flames as though wary of facing each other. They sat there in silence, sipping their coffee, aware of the unmistakable vibrations that occurred whenever they were in the same room. She wondered whether he felt them as strongly as she did.

Rafe turned around to pour himself another cup. "Thank you for allowing me back in the house. I wouldn't have blamed you if you'd thrown a rock and chased me away."

A dart of pain ran through her. "Rafe, don't." Her hand darted out, paused, then touched his. "There's no need for recriminations, you know. Believe me, I understand."

"I'm glad *you* do," he responded with bitterness, "because I left here wondering if I was going out of my mind. It has taken me this long to come to grips with my feelings." He settled back on the rug and faced her. "What I said to you that day was the truth as I saw it then."

"I know. I accepted it then and I have no reason not to accept it now." She sounded calm because that was the way she felt. She loved this man, the father of the child she was carrying, the lover she'd never dreamed existed before the past summer. Whatever his decision for them, she would accept it.

Rafe made an impatient gesture, running his hand through his hair. "I've tried to understand and, although it's no excuse, I recognize that I'd been pushing myself hard for several months." His smile flashed for a moment, then disappeared. "I was putting in very long hours in order to be able to return to Oregon. Even when I wasn't working, I couldn't sleep for thinking about you, wanting you.''

Ashley could feel the pain awakening within her, and she felt she had to get him to stop. She couldn't bear hearing that. ''Please, Rafe—''

His hand reached out and touched one of the curls lying on her shoulder. He picked it up as though measuring its weight, bounced it in his hand, then moved on to touch her shoulder.

She became very still at his touch, afraid that if she moved she'd throw herself into his arms. His nearness had started up all the old sensations once more. He had always affected her that way—she had no reason to believe it would ever change.

She started to remove his hand from her shoulder, when he suddenly grabbed her hand and carried it to his lips. He placed light, gentle kisses at the base of each finger, the thumb, and in the palm itself. He carefully folded her fingers over and placed her hand on the rug between them.

She turned her head away from the hypnotic flickering of the flames and watched as shadows danced across his face. Some of his color had faded, as though he'd spent the last months indoors.

''I knew I had to come and talk to you, share with you some of what I've discovered about myself these last few weeks.''

"I'm glad."

"You don't even know what I have to say," he said with a hint of confusion.

"That's true. I'm just glad that, whatever you have to say, you feel able to share it with me. I would like to think we might continue the friendship we began."

Pain shot across his face for a moment, then was gone. "I'm not surprised you feel that way, Ashley. As a husband and a lover I might manage to make a halfway decent friend."

"That isn't what I meant, Rafe, and you know it." She reached for his hand. "There's no reason for you to try to shoulder all the blame for the failure of our marriage. I'm willing to accept my part of it. Why should you feel guilty because it didn't work out?"

Rafe sat there watching her as the flames from the fireplace cast a gentle glow over her cheeks. She seemed so serene, somehow. Less tense, more content with her life. He had no reason to suppose she'd want him to step back into her life, but he had to find out. He couldn't continue wondering whether they might have had a chance together. "I wanted to talk to you tonight, Ashley, not about any mistake we made by getting married, but about my mistake in walking out."

Had she heard him right? What was he saying?

"I don't want to be just a friend of yours. I want to live here with you and love you, take care of you. I don't ever want to be separated from you again."

Her heart was hammering so loudly she was certain Rafe must hear it. How many nights had she dreamed that he had returned and was telling her just what she was hearing now? Surely she wasn't dreaming once again!

"But, Rafe, I'm still a lawyer. I can't change that, as much as I might want to try."

"I know that!" He started to reach for her, then stopped. "I discovered that we don't choose the person we fall in love with. We may think we do. We may think we know why we fell in love with that particular person. We can find all sorts of reasons to explain it." He raised her hand to his mouth and placed a feather kiss on her knuckles. "I had to face the fact that love wasn't something I could order about. When I fell in love with you, I didn't fall in love with just the indignant lady I first met or the passionate woman I came to know. I fell for the total person, everything that makes you what you are, and that includes your training and skill as a lawyer."

He stopped speaking, watching her face as she listened to him. Then he went on. "I can't sit here and apologize for what I said, because I meant it when I said it. I'm apologizing for being the kind of person who could set himself up to judge your behavior, to decide what kind of person you should be." He turned back to the fire. "I began to realize what kind of person *I* was and despised myself. I'll understand if you despise me as well."

"That isn't true, Rafe." She reached out and rested her hand on his sweater. She could feel his heart thudding.

"You threw all your time and energy into saving Raul's business while I stood on the sidelines condemning your methods." Ashley noted a roughness in his voice and glanced up in time to see a sheen of moisture in his eyes. She could feel his chest rise as he took a deep breath. "You gave me everything you had to give—your friendship, your love, your passion—and I threw it all back in your face and demanded more." The pain he felt broke through in his voice, and she could no longer stay silent.

"Rafe, we may not have any control over whom we love, but we can choose how we allow that love to affect us. I never wanted my love for you to form a cage to hold you against your will."

Tentatively Rafe placed his arm around Ashley's shoulders and pulled her against him. It felt so good to be close to him again. He kissed her just under her ear and muttered, "All I ever want is to be able to find myself snug within the confines of your love. That isn't a cage, dear heart; that would be heaven."

She turned her lips to his and gave him the answer he was almost afraid to expect. Finally, she pulled back and said, "I love you, Rafe. There's nothing you can do to stop me from loving you."

A shudder went through him and his arms tightened around her as he began to kiss her again. She pulled away once more, breathless, and laughed. "If you don't stop hugging me quite so fiercely, your son or daughter is going to punch you." Her face radiated the love she felt for him.

Rafe sat up, his face reflecting the emotions hitting him as her statement registered.

"Ashley?" He pushed her away and looked down at her body. His hand moved from her back to her stomach, where it rested on the slight protuberance. "You're pregnant," he announced in cautious tones.

"The doctor assures me that's the correct term for my condition."

"But, Ashley, why didn't you mention it? When did you— How—"

"Don't you dare ask me how it happened, or I'll show you just what kind of temper your wife has." Her glare didn't seem to intimidate him.

"When will it be here?"

"The doctor thinks the early part of May, from my rather vague information." She enjoyed watching his face, attempting to identify the emotions reflected there. A hint of concern, perhaps a touch of worry, then a flash of pride. Her smile faded as she saw the beginning of a frown.

"Why wasn't I told?" he demanded. Who said he wasn't arrogant? She supposed that arrogance was part of his makeup. If he could accept her choice of profession, she would overlook his overbearing ways—within reason, of course.

"I'm telling you now, Rafe." No tone of voice could have been more reasonable. His frown remained.

"That's because I came to you. When did you intend to tell me?" His accusation hung between them. She knew she'd better plead her case better than she'd ever done in a courtroom, or his resentment of the delay would remain between them. Before she could say any more, he got up from the rug and pulled her with gentle pressure toward him. "You shouldn't be sitting on the cold floor," he scolded as he sat down on the couch and pulled her onto his lap. Since she quite enjoyed that position, she didn't complain.

"Rafe, love, I'm going to have a baby. That doesn't call for treating me like an invalid."

She watched as a tide of red moved across his cheeks. "I know, but neither of us needs a cold. The floor's drafty."

"Of course." She hid her smile.

His face stern, his eyes serious, he repeated his question with a precision of speech that hinted at his suppressed emotions. "When did you intend to tell me?"

"I'm not sure. When I was more ready than I've felt up until now, I guess." He pulled her to him and began to kiss her along her cheekbone; then he pressed his lips to hers in a brief and wordless apology.

"Oh, Rafe." She put her arms around him. "I love you so."

"I have to expect a few unexplained quirks in your personality, I suppose. Besides, it's very comforting for me to know that." He leaned over and began to kiss her again. Between short kisses, he admitted, "Because—I don't know—what I'd do—if you didn't."

He picked her up and carried her down the hallway. The bedroom lamp was lit, casting a halo around the table on which it sat. He let her slide down his aroused body.

"Did you ask the doctor if I could make love to you?" He seemed to be having trouble with his breathing. Maybe he'd noticed the weight she had gained recently.

"No, because it didn't seem much of a possibility when I last saw him."

She watched Rafe mask his disappointment as he smiled and, in an offhand manner, suggested, ''Well, I think I'll hop into the shower. I may be a while, you just go ahead and get some rest. I won't disturb you when I come to bed.'' Ashley was impressed with his ability to appear nonchalant.

''Of course, the doctor didn't have to tell me anything. He gave me some books to read.'' She indicated the two on her nightstand. ''They say that at this stage it's safe for me to enjoy my marital relationship.'' Her eyes danced with mischief as she smiled up at him.

Rafe stood drinking in the expression on her face. Never had she seemed more beautiful. He loved her so much that he didn't know how to deal with it. He was afraid he would hurt her, he'd been without her for so long. He remembered those long, restless nights when his need for a woman had kept him awake. But he had known that it wasn't a need for just any woman, and he hadn't found the courage to face Ashley.

Ashley began to disrobe, and Rafe could see the beginning of a slight curve in her stomach. His baby. They'd never even discussed having children.

''Ashley?''

She pulled a heavy flannel gown over her head and looked at him. ''Yes?'' She looked like a little girl with ruffles around her neck and wrists and pink toes showing their tips under the ruffled hem.

"How do you feel about having a baby?"

Her radiant smile appeared once more. "I can hardly wait. I'll admit it was a bit of a shock at first, but I was excited even then."

"When did you find out?" He wished he'd been with her each day, every day, to watch her body change as his child grew within her.

"A few days before Raul's hearing." She hopped into bed, and set the dial of the electric blanket. "I forgot to ask you—do you sleep with an electric blanket?"

He paused, trying to adjust to the change in subject. "No, why?"

"Because I do, but there are dual controls, so you won't need to turn your side on."

"I suppose you think I'm going to sleep on one side of the bed and you'll be on the other?" He stood there with his hands on his hips, his snug pants leaving no doubt as to his condition.

"Well, maybe I won't need it tonight," she admitted a little breathlessly.

He rid himself of his clothes and crawled into bed beside her, managing to have most of her body touching him. He radiated enough heat for both of them, he knew. Returning to the previous subject, he asked, "Why didn't you tell me when I called?"

"I might have, if you hadn't told me you were coming up the next night. That's when I decided I should wait and tell you in person."

His hand slid down her leg until he found the ruffled hem, then it began the return journey against her bare skin until it came to rest at the top of her thigh.

"You didn't mention it the night I flew in," he reminded her.

Ashley's mind was not on the conversation. How could she possibly concentrate when his hand kept feathering across her abdomen and thigh. Just as she expected it to move closer to her inner thigh he would pause, then repeat his pattern.

She began to kiss him, trying to gain his entire attention. She knew she had succeeded when he took over the kiss. His tongue searched out all the hidden places within her mouth.

Ashley moaned. It had been so long. She didn't know how she'd managed to survive without his lovemaking.

When the kiss ended, Ashley was gasping for breath. Rafe continued the conversation as though nothing had interrupted them, as though his hand was not driving her crazy with its darting pattern of teasing maneuvers. "Why didn't you tell me when I flew up here?"

"Tell you what?" She'd forgotten what they had been talking about. She was too involved in relearning his body through the sensitive tips of her fingers. He'd lost weight. His body felt stripped of all surplus flesh—long, lean, and hungry. She could certainly identify with the hunger!

"That you were pregnant."

"Oh, Rafe." It took her a minute to try to think. That unbelievable feeling that Rafe managed to create in her was beginning its pulsating rhythm. His fingers had finally arrived at their destination and her hips arched with the rhythm of his touch. "I didn't tell you because we didn't do much talking that night." *And we're doing too much talking tonight!* "Love me, Rafe, please," she begged.

"I do, honey, indeed I do." She could hear the amusement in his voice. He had teased them both long enough. There would be plenty of time to catch up on the weeks they'd been apart. He recognized that there were a few things a person couldn't catch up on, but he certainly intended to do his best!

He pulled her gown up until she helped him to remove it. She no longer needed the gown to stay warm. Without the restriction of cloth between them, Rafe had unlimited freedom to love her body. He proceeded to show Ashley that she only thought she knew what lovemaking meant. He used his hands to touch her in ways she'd forgotten or never known. He used his tongue to trace the line of her breast, then to caress her until she thought she'd scream with the effort it took to hang on to her self-control. He used his mouth to chart each inch of her skin so that she was left quivering in his arms. He ran his hand reverently over the swelling that foretold the existence of their child, thankful she was the vessel he'd found to nurture his baby. Then he moved, poising himself over her, and gently eased himself to join her.

Rafe made the act of love more than bodies finding gratification. Their coming together became an act of healing. For the first time in their stormy relationship they were in complete harmony with each other. They could sense the other's need and fulfill it without verbal communication. They expressed their commitment and desire to spend the rest of their days and nights together, and as Ashley drifted into a fulfilled, satisfying sleep she remembered that they'd never discussed his career or hers, or where they might live and how.

For the first time in their relationship each acknowledged that those issues were unimportant compared with the one crucial fact—they belonged together. Everything else could be worked out.

Chapter Eleven

The smell of coffee wafted into Ashley's consciousness, and she tried to shake the sleep from her brain. She was tired, and her body felt like a football field that had been used for heavy scrimmages.

She managed to open her eyes partway and squinted to see the clock. Her bedside table was gone. In its place sat a French provincial table holding a lamp with a ruffled shade. This was not her bedroom. She shifted gingerly in the bed and spied Rafe as he stood by the window. The morning sun slanted through the blinds.

She smiled. How could she have forgotten? Rafe stood there studying the tiny face that was the only thing showing from the pink bundle he held. His awed expression held her silent and she watched him as he examined the tiny nose, which looked more like a button than a human appendage, the delicate ears tucked neatly against a well-shaped head, and the wispy hair that clung in soft curls around a beautiful face. They were in the birthing room of a San Francisco hospital where, during the early hours of the previous night, their daughter had been born.

Her mind drifted over the months that had passed, and her eyelids fluttered closed once more as she remembered them.

She had never told Rafe the real reason for her leaving the law firm in Portland. Her explanation mentioned different philosophies, an inability to communicate, a mutual decision by everyone concerned. She had no idea he would be so upset until he explained his intention to relocate in Oregon. They had spent many long hours discussing their future together, and she was surprised at Rafe's insistence that she continue her career.

She knew she could never walk away from that part of her life. Too many years had been dedicated to acquiring the skills she had. But her timetable no longer seemed important or necessary.

Rafe took her with him to San Francisco, and she finally realized the wealth of the man she had married. His condominium sat on one of the famous hills overlooking the bay. Her entire house could easily have nestled in a corner of his apartment. They spent their time like tourists, or perhaps like tourists on a honeymoon.

However, Ashley knew that Rafe was right. She could no more ignore the lawyer in her than she could the wife and mother.

Her eyes fluttered open as she thought, *And I managed to have the best of both worlds.* A casual phone conversation with a friend from law school opened doors Ashley never knew existed.

"Ashley!" Susan had exclaimed. "It's good to hear from you. How long will you be in town?"

That question prompted myriad explanations about a new husband and a new residence.

"You mean you quit your job in Portland?" Susan knew how important the position had been to Ashley. Because she trusted her friend, Ashley explained exactly what had happened and almost enjoyed the explosion of her reaction.

"My God, Ashley, those people must be throwbacks to some prehistoric time. Have you checked any of their pulses lately? They must be fossilized by now."

Ashley couldn't answer for a moment because she was laughing. At last she managed to say, "Oh, Susan, you're so good for me. The reason I called was to see if you'll be free for lunch one of these days."

They made a date, and when they met Susan had some astounding information to pass on. "I told a couple of the partners in our firm about you, including the fact you were on the *Law Review*," she added with a wink, "and a little of what happened in Portland." She stopped, her green eyes flashing with excitement. "And guess what?"

"I give up—what?"

"They want to meet you. They want to know if you intend to take the California bar exams, how much time you intend to give to work, both now and after the baby—"

"You mentioned that I was pregnant?"

"Of course. Why not? It doesn't affect how your mind works, does it? Anyway—"

"Oh, Susan, I can't believe this. Are you telling me they would consider hiring me?"

"Yes, dear friend, that's exactly what I'm telling you. They want to set up an interview with you. What do you think?"

Ashley had sat back in her chair with a sigh. "I think I'm dreaming."

As she shifted once more in the bed, she recalled that interview and the subsequent offer of employment. After she talked it over with Rafe, they had decided that she would wait until the fall to start working again, on a limited basis. Once again Rafe surprised her by his insistence on taking an active part in raising their offspring. He would plan his schedule around hers, and she would do the same with his, so that the baby would have at least one loving parent with her at all times.

Rafe had embraced the role of father-to-be with zeal. Raul pointed out that it was only because Rafe had thought he was too old to become a father and the shock had unhinged him. Only a much-loved brother could have cast such a slur against Rafe's manhood and survived.

Not only had Rafe read both books Ashley's doctor had recommended, he had also checked out other books from the library, in case he might have missed something.

As soon as they had decided to stay in California, Rafe had insisted on finding the best specialist around, made an appointment, and escorted Ashley to the doctor's office, even sitting in on part of the consultation.

It was Rafe who had insisted on attending childbirth classes. He had adopted the same attitude toward the classes and her pregnancy as he did everything else. He investigated thoroughly, read everything he could find on the subject, and could probably have conducted the class himself had the teacher suddenly fallen into a fit. Ashley thought it was no wonder he made a success of everything he tackled; he probably wore out everyone else.

"Good morning," Ashley murmured, her voice still husky from sleep. Rafe glanced up from the baby, then moved over to the chair by her bed and sat down.

"How are you feeling this morning?" His face still showed traces of the anxiety of the previous night.

"Oh, I'm just fine, love. Were you able to get some sleep?"

"A few hours," he admitted. "I managed to wake your folks with the news that after all those grandsons they now have a girl in the family." He took her hand in his and pressed it against his cheek, an endearing gesture that never failed to touch her.

"Were you sorry we had a girl?"

He looked surprised at the question. "Of course not. I placed an order for a girl just like you." He smiled. "And she is—she's beautiful."

He must be looking at her through the eyes of love. When the nurse had helped Ashley to feed the baby, she'd taken a good look at her daughter. If you could call wrinkled skin and wisps of black hair beautiful, then yes, Ashley guessed she was. She knew she'd never felt such a fierce love as she had when she held the tiny scrap in her arms. Motherhood had some definite pleasures that could be found in no other role.

"Did you call Raul and Jeanine?"

"Of course. I told them I hoped to have you home in the next day or two. They said they'd fly down over the weekend if you thought you'd be up to company by then." Rafe's eyes were still shadowed with concern. Ashley's labor had lasted several hours. Rafe hadn't realized when he attended the classes how different it would be to see Ashley hurting, and when he saw that first hard pain hit her, he wasn't sure he could handle his reaction. Their training had helped, and now, as he looked at the tiny infant, he knew he wouldn't have missed her arrival for anything.

As he watched, his tiny daughter wriggled and stretched her fingers wide, then curled them into minuscule fists once more.

Hesitantly Rafe asked, "Would you mind if we call her Teresa?"

"That's a lovely name, Rafe. If that's what you want to name her, we will."

"That was my grandmother's name. She was one of my favorite people in the whole world when I was young."

"When you were young*er*. You're still young, love."

"Not after last night. I'm not sure about having a second one."

"I am," Ashley responded in a serious tone. "I think it's important to raise children together. You know my feelings about an only child."

Rafe's smile gleamed white against his dark skin. "Yes, ma'am. I'll do my best to oblige you, ma'am. Just let me know when you're ready, ma'am."

"You can cut out the fake accent, Tex. Nobody's buying it."

The nurse came in to check on mother and child, and Rafe left Ashley to rest.

She woke up in the afternoon to find Rafe sitting by her bed, watching her with a tender expression.

"Why didn't you wake me up?"

"You're going to need all the rest you can get. I have a hunch Miss Teresa is going to keep you hopping once we get you two home." He leaned over and placed a kiss on her mouth. "By the way, Tasha and I had a nice long discussion this morning."

"Omigosh, I'd forgotten all about her."

"So she told me. As a matter of fact, she made it clear she did not approve of my arriving home at dawn this morning without you. So she tried her hand at a little redecorating."

"Oh, no! What did she do?" Visions of some of his original oil paintings with claw marks on them danced through her head.

"She found a box of tissues, shredded them, and distributed them through several of the rooms. It was quite colorful."

"Oh, Rafe. Maybe we'd better give her away, especially now that Teresa is here."

"No way. Tasha has agreed to accept Teresa, and I intend to see that she does. You know you could never get rid of her."

If he'd spent the morning picking up tiny scraps of shredded tissues and could still sound so agreeable, Ashley knew she had no need to worry about Rafe's patience.

By the time Raul and Jeanine arrived, Ashley and Teresa were home and a routine of sorts had been established. Rafe's prediction proved right. Tasha did an admirable job of ignoring the new addition.

After examining the sleeping infant and returning to the living room, Jeanine exclaimed, "You're certainly spry this soon after giving birth."

Raul answered for Ashley. "That's probably because she didn't gain a lot of weight during her pregnancy like some people we know."

Jeanine's nose rose in the air. "The doctor said I was just right. You were the only one complaining."

"Just right for having a baby elephant, maybe."

Ashley watched as an accent pillow sailed through the air and decided it was time to change the subject. "What's new in Oregon? The California news media seem to think the world ceases to exist at the northern state border."

"Pete Wilson was convicted on several counts." Jeanine paused, her forehead wrinkled. "I can't remember all the charges, but it was enough to keep him out of the way for a few years."

"That should have hurt Tysinger's case," Ashley responded.

Raul, stretched out in one of the lounge chairs, spoke up. "It didn't help, but he's got some wily lawyers. I have a feeling they'll keep him from being brought to trial as long as they can find one more technicality to pull out of the books."

"Have you had any more problems at the plant since the hearing last fall?" Rafe moved over and sat down next to Ashley, sliding his arm around her.

"Nothing. Jackson turned in his resignation, but I refused to take it. He's a good man and I don't expect anything similar to happen ever again." Ashley was glad to see that the subject could be discussed without creating any tension. All of that seemed to have happened in another lifetime and had little to do with the life she had established in the past few months.

Later that night Ashley finished breast-feeding Teresa and crawled into bed next to Rafe. The doctor had suggested nursing for the first few weeks, and she enjoyed the closeness with her tiny daughter.

"Rafe?"

"Hmm?"

"Are you asleep?"

"I was. Why?"

"Oh, nothing. I was just thinking of Tysinger."

He pulled her over so that her head rested on his chest, enjoying the feel of her curves once again. "What about him?"

"Do you really think he's guilty?"

"You bet I do, and so do most of the law-enforcement agencies. The catch is to prove it."

"I can't help but remember that if it hadn't been for Tysinger I might never have met you." She moved her hand lightly across his waist.

She could feel his chuckle deep in his chest. "That's true, my love, but somehow I don't feel like sending him a thank-you note."

She leaned on her elbow and stared down at him. "I can understand that. You would still be a happily single man if it hadn't been for him. It's a wonder you haven't insisted that he be placed behind bars for life!"

A glow of tenderness lit Rafe's eyes, and he placed his palm against her cheek, then stroked her jaw line and her neck. "Ashley, I never knew what happiness was until I married—"

Her heart melted at his admission.

"—but of course by then it was too late!"

"Rafe!"

He began to laugh at the expression on her face. Pulling her to him, he gave her a kiss that left no doubt how he felt about her. When he finally let her go, he grinned.

"Now, quit fishing for compliments and get some rest. Otherwise your daughter is going to have a grumpy mama trying to feed her in a few hours." He cupped his hand around her breast. "I'm afraid I can't offer to feed her like I did Josh."

He was right. There was no need for soul-searching. Despite the odds, their marriage was working in a most satisfying manner. With a sigh of contentment, Ashley curled up beside her warm husband and fell asleep.

* * * * *

Harlequin Romance ®

Delightful

Affectionate

Romantic

Emotional

Tender

Original

Daring

Riveting

Enchanting

Adventurous

Moving

Harlequin Romance—the
series that has it all!

HROM-G

HARLEQUIN PRESENTS

HARLEQUIN PRESENTS
men you won't be able to resist falling in love with...

HARLEQUIN PRESENTS
women who have feelings just like your own...

HARLEQUIN PRESENTS
powerful passion in exotic international settings...

HARLEQUIN PRESENTS
intense, dramatic stories that will keep you turning
to the very last page...

HARLEQUIN PRESENTS
The world's bestselling romance series!

Harlequin® Historical

If you're a serious fan of historical romance,
then you're in luck!

Harlequin Historicals brings you
stories by bestselling authors, rising new stars
and talented first-timers.

Ruth Langan & Theresa Michaels
Mary McBride & Cheryl St. John
Margaret Moore & Merline Lovelace
Julie Tetel & Nina Beaumont
Susan Amarillas & Ana Seymour
Deborah Simmons & Linda Castle
Cassandra Austin & Emily French
Miranda Jarrett & Suzanne Barclay
DeLoras Scott & Laurie Grant…

You'll never run out of favorites.

Harlequin Historicals…they're too good to miss!

HH-GEN

LOOK FOR OUR FOUR FABULOUS MEN!

Each month some of today's bestselling authors bring
four new fabulous men to Harlequin American Romance.
Whether they're rebel ranchers, millionaire power brokers
or sexy single dads, they're all gallant princes—and
they're all ready to sweep you into lighthearted fantasies
and contemporary fairy tales where anything is possible
and where all your dreams come true!

You don't even have to make a wish...Harlequin American
Romance will grant your every desire!

Look for Harlequin American Romance wherever Harlequin
books are sold!

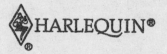

Frank Sinatra
and
Mia Farrow

When Frank Sinatra became involved with Mia Farrow, she was nineteen, and he was pushing fifty. He had two children older than his new love. Mia's career was just starting to take off from her role in "Peyton Place" when Frank rented a yacht for a month-long vacation with Mia. The script writers for "Peyton Place" wrote her character into a coma; if she and Frank married and she decided to give up her career, her character could then conveniently die. But at the end of the voyage, the press headlines read "Mia Not Mrs. Yet." Shortly after, however, Frank bought Mia a nine-carat engagement ring. Remembering that Sinatra had broken up with Lauren Bacall when she told the press she and Sinatra were engaged, Mia claimed the jewel was a "friendship ring," but on July 19, 1966, the couple married in a four-minute civil ceremony in Las Vegas.

B-FRANK